SOMETIME[illegible] [illegible]T EVEN THE BE[illegible] [illegible]. . .

Ginger poured herself [illegible] n stood sipping it, sizing Terry up. She still [illegible], but loosely, almost as if she'd forgotten about it. Terry stared back, still in her racing silks soaked with sweat, her dusty boots sinking into the plush carpet. Finally Ginger spoke.

"So what do you think I should do with you for mouthing off to me like that?"

Terry decided to play it a little dangerous. "Maybe you should teach me a lesson I won't forget."

"Oh, so you think you're ready to play with the grown-ups now, do you?"

"Who says I'm playing?"

"I say. I say when you're playing and when you're not. Maybe you forgot who owns you?"

Again Ginger's words made Terry forget any danger in her desire to show Ginger once and for all that nobody owned her. Without thinking, she covered the ground between them and grasped the ends of the long silk scarf that hung around Ginger's neck as if she were going to rein in an unruly horse. She thought about tightening the scarf until Ginger begged for mercy, but instead she found herself tugging on it just enough to bring Ginger's mouth to hers. Then they were in the bedroom, and Terry showed Ginger that Silky wasn't the only one she could get to the finish line . . .

The Big Book of Lesbian Horse Stories

Alisa Surkis
and
Monica Nolan

Kensington Books
http://www.kensingtonbooks.com

KENSINGTON BOOKS are published by

Kensington Publishing Corp.
850 Third Avenue
New York, NY 10022

All Kensington titles, imprints, and distributed lines are available at special quantity discounts for bulk purchases for sales promotions, premiums, fund-raising, and educational or institutional use.

Special book excerpts or customized printings can also be created to fit specific needs. For details, write or phone the office of the Kensington Special Sales Manager: Kensington Publishing Corp., 850 Third Avenue, New York, NY 10022. Attn. Special Sales Department. Phone: 1-800-221-2647.

ISBN 0-7582-0254-7

First Trade Printing: October 2002
10 9 8 7 6 5 4 3 2 1

Printed in the United States of America

For Julie Ann and Colleen

Contents

Village Girl

Jean could practically smell the freshly mowed hay. It was the last week of June now. This was always Jean's favorite time on the farm. Everything was just bursting with life then. June was when she'd ride Cracker to that little hollow below the creek and just lie back in the wildflowers that were starting to burst through and look up at the sky and think. Think about all sorts of things—how the crops looked, if she'd go to college next year, if Buddy was okay over in Vietnam. She'd think about Ma and Pa. And she'd think about Cathy . . .

"Say, Jean, you planning on pouring those drinks sometime tonight?"

Jean snapped back to reality. She was holding a cocktail shaker in her hand, and the fresh-mowed hay was only the new air freshener Tony was trying in the bathroom.

"Be patient, ladies. Is there someplace else you need to be?"

There was wry laughter from the three drag queens at the bar, as Jean agitated the cocktail shaker with a practiced gesture, then poured out the three pink ladies, tossing a paper umbrella into each drink with unerring accuracy.

"So, Jean, which girl has your head in the clouds today? Dorothy? Or is it Allison now?" Carmen asked, with a wink to her friends.

"You're behind the times, Carmen. I broke up with Allison this morning. All I have is this little memento." She dipped into her pocket and pulled out the macramé wallet she had attached to the end of her long key chain. She smiled fondly, recalling Allison, her soulful brown eyes, her bell-bottomed jeans, the strange poetry she used to read aloud in Washington Square Park. She claimed to see deep into Jean's soul, but Jean didn't want anyone looking at her soul, and so it had ended.

"What did you get from Dorothy?" Carmen asked, fluttering her false eyelashes at her companions. The friendly drag queen had taken Jean under her wing when the big farm girl had first arrived in New York a week ago, picking the hayseeds out of her hair, and Carmen took pride in showing off how far Jean had come. Jean shook her head at the thought—had she really ever been that young and naive?

"Well, I guess I owe Dorothy for this." Jean smoothed her dark hair, slicked back into a perfect D.A., with a hint of Elvis Presley pompadour. Dorothy operated a beauty salon in Queens. She was quite a bit older than Jean, and had taught her a lot more than how to style her hair. But even she couldn't teach Jean how to forget Cathy—or Cracker.

"You're quite the lady killer," one of Carmen's friends teased. "I bet you left a trail of broken hearts back home."

Jean's face darkened as she said with a bitter laugh,

"Only if you count mine." One of the girls started to reply, but Jean abruptly turned away and started in on the pile of dirty glasses in the bar sink. "Back home" was someplace she didn't like to think about. Behind her, she could hear snatches of Carmen's whispered explanation, ". . . home-coming queen . . . caught in the hollow . . . horse killed . . ." She knew that Carmen was trying to save her from having to answer any more questions, but each phrase she heard was like a dagger through her heart.

Jean was relieved when Tony returned from cooking the accounts in the back office. He slipped behind the bar, gesturing with his thumb toward the front door. "Back to your post, kid," he said. It was Jean's job to keep an eye on the door. When the police showed up, she was the one to send the warning by flicking the lights. She started to head toward the front, when she heard Tony calling her back, "Wait a second, kid. Run downstairs and get a fresh keg first."

Jean was hoisting the keg to her shoulder when she heard a sudden silence, as the jukebox stopped, and then a menacing rumble of voices. A raid! Gently she set the keg back down and peered out the tiny barred window at the parade of feet going from bar to paddy wagon. Jean knew that if everyone cooperated and the police were in a good mood that night, most folks would just have to suffer through a few hours down at Centre Street. Maybe this would be one of those good nights. She heard Tony's voice from above, "I thought you guys were coming before the evening rush! You're killing my business, you know that?" There would be no more work tonight and Jean was glad. She wanted no more reminders of home, of Cathy.

But even that brief mention of Cathy had stirred Jean up, and she had learned since coming to the city that other women could satisfy the hunger that Cathy had awakened.

She headed over to the Colony. As the door swung closed behind her, she let her eyes travel around the room. There was Dorothy, with Frankie; Allison wasn't here tonight, but that sad-eyed girl at the bar was the same type. And there was Marcie, the first girl she'd slept with when she got to New York. Jean shuddered as she saw the plaintive look in Marcie's eyes—a look that promised unwanted complications. But she needed someone tonight, someone to slake the desire she felt growing inside her, someone to obliterate the past—someone who was nothing like Cathy, or Cracker.

Then she saw her. The woman stood up from a table in the corner, and sauntered over to the jukebox. From the long black mane of hair to the red high-heeled shoes, she was all woman. Her black sheath fit her like a glove, accentuating her full bosom. She glanced over at Jean, just once, but it was enough to let Jean know that it was for her, the seductive roll of her hips as she walked across the floor, the flash of leg through the slit in her skirt. She was nothing like Cathy—or Cracker—and she was everything Jean wanted—at least for that night.

It was many drinks later, and Jean had learned the woman's name—Louise—and seen in her eyes a need that matched Jean's own. "Let's go, baby," was all she needed to say, and the woman rose instantly and put her hand on Jean's arm.

Then they were at an old factory building on the west side of town, riding a big metal cage up, up, and up. "What kind of person lives here?" Jean asked as she trailed her fingers down Louise's back.

"An artist, baby. I'm a sculptor, and I need a lot of space."

And then they were inside the loft, and there was a lot of space, filled with huge sculptures made out of wood and scrap metal. Louise laughed suddenly and, dropping her coat, she darted through the loft and hid behind a statue. "Hide and seek!" Her voice sounded eerie in the semi-darkness, amid the looming shapes and shadows of her strange sculptures. Then she stepped into a square of light from the window. She had stripped off her black sheath and was clad only in a slip. Jean took her into her arms, and kissed her for the first time, a searing kiss, which seemed to melt them together, like two different kinds of metal forming a new amalgam. The woman leaned back on one of the sculptures, and instinctively, Jean straddled her quivering body. As Jean stared, the abstract shape of this sculpture seemed to take on an almost recognizable form. "What's this supposed to be?" Jean murmured as she pulled the strap of the slip down over Louise's shoulder. Jean's mouth moved swiftly downward, until Louise's breast was in her mouth and she could feel the hard pink bud between her teeth.

"Well, the short answer is that it's a horse," Louise said, her breath coming in panting gasps. She gave a sudden moan as Jean unintentionally bit down. *Horse!* The word jangled sharply in Jean's ear. But Louise didn't notice Jean's agitation and the bite only aroused her even further. "That's right, baby," she panted. "Ride me!"

No! No more riding! Wild-eyed, Jean dismounted the voluptuous figure. She turned away, unable to meet Louise's puzzled brown eyes—how could she have failed to notice how like Cracker's they were? Jean ran from the loft, trying to escape the memories that had begun to surface. Like a crazy kaleidoscope, she saw in her mind's eye jagged images—Cracker on his side—blood on her own hands—Cathy crying, her blouse unbuttoned.

When she arrived at the Colony, flushed, panting, she'd recovered some of her equilibrium. Dorothy was gone, and so was Marcie, but the sad-eyed girl at the bar was still there, nursing a beer. Jean headed right to her. "What do you know about horses?" she demanded harshly.

The girl looked bewildered. "Horses? Why noth—" Before she could finish her sentence, Jean had covered the girl's mouth with her own.

Much later, Jean awoke in yet another darkened apartment, her head pounding. She pulled herself out of bed, remembering Dorothy's admonition, "The first hangover's always the worst. After that, you get used to 'em." At the time Jean hadn't believed her, but that had been days ago. The slight girl sprawled on the bed began to stir, and Jean quickly slipped out of the apartment. In the chilly, predawn light Jean lit a cigarette and shivered. It was both too late and too early to go back to the little room she rented over Luigi's Ristorante.

She turned and walked downtown, hands stuffed deep in her jeans pockets. Her thoughts turned to her arrival in New York, fresh from the farm and filled with pain. All she'd known about girls like her was from a paperback she'd gotten at the Doylestown drugstore. In that book, the lesbians had lived in Greenwich Village, so as soon as Jean got off the Greyhound, that was where she'd headed. Jean tried not to think about last night in Louise's apartment as she recalled how the girl in the story had gone crazy at the end. After all, Jean consoled herself, the book had been wrong about other things. The girls in the story had all worn Bermuda shorts and knee socks. What a shock it had been to arrive in New York and find the Village bars filled with chinos and blue jeans!

There had been a lot to learn those first few days and it had been hard for Jean. Growing up, she couldn't remember a year when she didn't win at least three blue ribbons at the county fair, but in the Village nobody cared about the quickest way to fatten a pig, or the best crop to rotate with corn. Suddenly Jean had found herself on the asking side of all the questions. How her new friends would laugh when she asked, "What's reefer?" or "What's a daisy chain?" Then there'd been that little problem she had telling the difference between femmes and drag queens—though at least she'd gotten to know Carmen and the rest of the gang that way. And she'd learned fast—real fast. Soon *she* was warning the new butch to watch out she didn't get flipped by that pretty "femme" who was actually kiki.

While her thoughts roamed, Jean had wandered far downtown, to a part of Manhattan she'd never visited before. Dawn was breaking, and as it grew lighter, her nose twitched suspiciously. Freshly mowed hay, again! Was her mind playing tricks on her? She was in the middle of Manhattan, wasn't she? Then there came a shrill whinny, and Jean felt a rush of fear and longing. The nickering came again, the unmistakable sound of a horse in distress.

Instinctively Jean followed the sound, around the corner to a big stable on a dead-end street. As she peered down a passageway between two rows of stalls, she saw a horse on cross-ties, ears pinned back, trying to rear up. Jean stood for a moment, watching in horror as the groom grabbed one of the cross-ties and tried to haul the horse's head down.

"Chopper!" he snarled. "Settle down—settle down, damn you!"

Jean wanted desperately to help, but her feet were frozen to the ground by the bitter voice inside her that asked how she could hope to help this horse when she had been powerless to help Cracker?

Muttering to himself, the groom bent, picked up a riding crop and began striking Chopper across his poll. Jean's hesitation vanished as she watched this horse straining against his ties to avoid the blows, eyes rolling in terror. Cracker was gone, but this horse was alive and Jean had to stop his pain. Pushing the groom aside, she snatched up a cloth, and dipping it in the bucket of cold water, she laid it on the horse's scarred pasterns.

"Can't you see this horse has had bone spavins?" she spat at the groom. "Someone must have blistered his pasterns!"

"This horse's got a bad attitude, just like you, ya nosy little squirt—get the hell out of here!"

Jean clenched her fists and stood her ground. Just being near a horse opened the wound she was trying to heal, but she couldn't walk away. The groom moved toward her, brandishing the riding crop, and Jean raised her arm to fend off the impending blows. Suddenly a voice commanded, "Stop it! Stop it right now!"

Turning, Jean saw a woman limping toward them as fast as she could. She had a face Jean trusted instantly, full of freckles and framed by crinkly red hair, cut short. She might have been Jean's age, except for the lines around her bright blue eyes that betrayed her years. As soon as she reached them, she turned to the scowling groom.

"Tommy, you're paid to groom these horses, not beat them! That's it! You're fired!"

"I'm a city employee," the man said smugly. "This has to go through the union!"

"It will," the woman responded. "You can sit at home collecting your pay for the next year so far as I care, but you're not stepping a foot on these premises again!"

Tommy stared at the woman, then wheeled angrily and walked away. The woman watched Tommy's retreating back, and then turned to Jean, scratched her brow for a moment, and said with a grin, "Want a job?"

Jean stared back, dumbfounded. Standing here, surrounded by horses, with Chopper nuzzling her neck—it all felt so right. Chopper lowered his head and nudged at Jean's side and Jean instinctively reached into her jacket pocket and pulled out a lump of sugar. She must have put that there the last time she went out with Cracker. Once more the past rose up before her eyes—the loud crack, then Cracker falling, whinnying in pain, the blood, and a blood-spattered Cathy looking on in horror. Could she let herself be near horses again? Stalling, she asked, "Whose horses are these?"

The woman pointed up at a sign over the entryway as she replied, "These are the New York Police Stables. Mounted Policewoman Midge O'Brien, at your service. So how about it?"

Jean's thoughts of reentering the world of horses were doused with cold water. She thought about the raids, about the times her friends would show up at the bar the next day with a black eye or a broken arm. Jean knew it was only a matter of time before she ended up in a paddy wagon. Back in Doylestown she'd really believed all that business about serving and protecting. Sheriff Taylor had even been a friend of the family. Then came that last night when he showed up at the house to warn her that if she didn't steer clear of Cathy, she'd find herself in jail.

Jean's throat tightened. "I'm not interested in working with horses," she said quickly.

Midge looked quizzically at Jean. "Won't you reconsider? I've been trying to get rid of Tommy for months, but I could never come up with a suitable replacement." Midge added with a wink, " 'Til now!"

"I'm telling you, you've got the wrong woman," said Jean desperately. She knew that now was the time to walk away, but she couldn't quite yet. Something held her in that peaceful stable. "What happened to your leg?" she asked, trying to change the subject.

The blue eyes darkened and looked away. "Trouble on the job," Midge managed to get out before something caught in her throat.

Jean waited awkwardly, while Midge collected herself.

"Couple weeks back, me and Lucky, that's my . . . that was my partner, we went by a liquor store just as it was being robbed." Midge turned away for a moment. When she turned back, she resumed her story in clipped tones. "The perpetrator fled the scene of the crime and Lucky and I pursued him. We cornered him in a blind alley and I ordered the perp to surrender. He drew a weapon and shot." Again Midge paused. "The bullet would have hit me, but Lucky reared up and took the bullet himself. We went down with Lucky on top, and I ended up with a sprained ankle." Midge gestured at her leg.

"And Lucky?" Jean asked.

"Lucky wasn't so lucky," said Midge, her voice rough with emotion. "He never got up again. I'm officially off duty until my ankle heals up, but I spend most of my time down here, getting to know Chopper. He's my new partner."

Jean didn't know what to say. This woman had lost her horse too, yet here she was, preparing to go back on the streets on a new mount. There was a courage to it that Jean had to admire. Chopper blew out his breath in a comfortable snort, and the sound went straight to Jean's heart. She looked at the horse, a tall light-colored chestnut with a white blaze down his face. Something in his sensitive, intelligent eyes made her feel as if she'd found a kindred spirit.

"You know, I'm kind of in the lurch, now that I've fired Tommy," Midge said, watching Jean look at Chopper. "Me and my redheaded temper! You'd help me out a lot if you could fill in—just temporarily, of course."

Something in Jean that she could not control made her respond, "Well . . . just temporarily."

The Stonewall Inn was hopping that night, and Jean had trouble keeping her eyes open as she sat on her stool by the door. Tony wrinkled his nose in disgust as he walked by. "Jean! Who the hell you hanging out with these days? You stink, kid."

"Sorry, Tony," Jean mumbled, embarrassed.

"What, are you fishing in the gutter these days? You used to run with such nice girls."

Jean stopped herself from explaining. Better let Tony, let them all think the smell of the stables that lingered on her was the result of a sordid affair. Jean knew they could never understand her working for the police, any more than someone like Midge could ever understand Jean's Village life.

Jean had spent most of that afternoon working with Chopper. Midge had stayed around, making easy conversation. Despite her reservations, Jean found herself enjoying both Midge's company and the horse's.

"I thought I knew a lot about horses, but you're a real expert," Midge had said admiringly at one point. Jean remembered the warm feeling it had given her.

"So, how'd you get into police work?" Jean had asked, hoping to find some way to reconcile her growing fondness for Midge with Midge's career choice.

"Never thought about doing anything else," Midge had responded. "It's what my pop did, all my brothers. Family tradition."

Jean had digested that in silence as she reached down to pick out one of Chopper's back hooves. That was when she'd seen them. All along the back of Chopper's legs were tiny scars, and Jean knew what they were from. Someone had tried to make a jumper out of Chopper, smacking his legs with a spiked two by four to make him jump higher.

"That's why he's so skittish," Midge had said softly after Jean had explained.

"He was probably never meant to be a jumper—you can't make a horse into something he isn't meant to be!" Jean had burst out. "With his balance, poise, and elegant step, he should have been trained for dressage!"

"Well, he's safe now," Midge had said. "I'm sure we can make him happy here. Besides, I've always thought dressage was kind of a sissy style."

But as Jean sat on the stool, thinking about Chopper, she wondered if being a police horse was the best thing for him. A police horse needed steady nerves, and with all his fine qualities, Chopper didn't have those. And it troubled her, what Midge had said about dressage. Why did she have to judge like that?

"Honey, I have a surprise for you." Carmen kissed her on both cheeks, and handed her a beer. "A friend of yours is here to see you." Jean looked up to see Louise coming toward her as Carmen dropped her voice a few octaves and added, "I explained about the horse trauma and she's not mad." As Jean watched the raven-haired beauty approach, she felt again the desire of the night before. Somehow, Jean knew that the horse sculpture couldn't hurt her anymore.

Carmen continued in an excited whisper, "Now you hang on to this one—she's very talented, has all sorts of connections to the art scene, not to mention a very wealthy family out on Long Island." Jean smiled at Carmen's mothering, and then shooed her away as Louise reached them. Jean didn't need a mother to tell her what to do now. As she felt Louise's lips burning into her own, her body recalled the unfulfilled passions of last night. Closing time couldn't come soon enough.

Jean sat up in bed, wondering what time it was. She was in a strange bed under a scarlet comforter. Finally she spotted a small clock on top of an orange crate. The hands pointed to 9:30—and she'd told Midge she'd get to the stables at 10:00! She wanted to work Chopper as much as possible, to steady him before Midge started taking him out. Hurriedly, she grabbed her clothes and headed for the bathroom.

"Morning," called a voice when she emerged. She made her way through the forest of sculptures until she came upon a small kitchen in the corner of the loft, where Louise was pouring mugs of coffee.

"I'm sorry, Louise, I've got to run," she began.

"I'm sure you have time for coffee," said Louise with a wide smile. She handed the steaming brew to Jean.

Jean eyed Louise as she sipped her coffee. Her hair was piled up on her head this morning in a kind of bird's nest tangle, with paintbrushes stuck through to hold it in place. Louise's next words caught Jean off guard.

"So this horse thing of yours—I understand *perfectly* what you're going through. I've been in psychoanalysis for years and my analyst is an expert in this sort of thing." Jean listened with interest as Louise told her about the intricate theory which explained the ties between lesbians and horses. Jean admired Louise's openness, but she still couldn't talk about what had happened that day in the hollow. It was too painful. Instead she wondered aloud about the complex psychological drives that had led them to their unconventional lifestyle. Louise listened knowingly as Jean told her how Pa had taught her to run the tractor and how Ma would never let Jean into the kitchen until she'd wiped the mud off her shoes. Finally, Louise just smiled and shrugged her shoulders. "I don't know. Sometimes I wonder why we even have to ask these questions."

It was nice talking like this, but as much as Jean liked Louise, she knew it couldn't last. It could never last—not as long as Cathy still had a hold on her heart. Jean knew there would never be another love like Cathy. It was time to make her usual speech. "Louise, you're an awfully great girl, and we've had a wonderful time, but I'm not much for domesticity—"

"Neither am I," said Louise. "It's really too bourgeois!"

"What I'm trying to tell you, Louise," Jean continued, "I'm not the settling-down type."

Louise just laughed and shook her head. "Help yourself to more coffee. I have to meet my friend Andy—I told him I'd help him with his movie. Make sure the door latches behind you."

Jean and Midge spent the morning putting Chopper through his paces, with Midge in the saddle and Jean keeping a close eye out for any of Chopper's antics that might threaten Midge's bad ankle. Jean admired Midge's firm, yet gentle manner with Chopper. Midge might be wrong about Chopper's future as a police horse, but she was a fine horsewoman, no question. From remarks Midge let drop, about rapists apprehended and lost children restored to their parents, Jean began to see that Midge was quite different from the kind of policemen she'd come to know working at the Stonewall.

Jean's admiration for Midge had not stopped there. Midge had arrived at the stables straight from the precinct, where she'd been filling out paperwork, still in her crisp blue uniform. The uniform, which was so repellent on the men who raided the bar, had a strangely unsettling effect on Jean. She found herself noticing the swell of Midge's breasts beneath the shiny brass buttons and the way the holster rested on Midge's full hips. From the first, Jean had suspected that Midge and she had more in common than just horses, and now she had to know. But how to find out in this straight world, where she had to watch her words?

"Midge, have you ever had a best friend?" Jean began.

"Well, sure. All kids have best friends."

"What about when you weren't a kid anymore? Did you ever have a friend then who was just . . . somehow . . . special?"

"I've certainly known a lot of people in my life who were very special," Midge responded carefully.

Frustrated, Jean dropped the topic. What was she thinking—even if Midge was a lesbian, she was clearly butch, and Jean bridled at the thought that she might be kiki. But she'd learned to look at so many things differently in the last week that she began to wonder if these roles really mattered.

As she lay in bed that night, smelling the garlic wafting up from Luigi's below, Jean felt a new kind of hope growing within her. She was learning to be around horses again, and she'd made some new friends: first Chopper, and then Midge and Louise. Maybe she'd go back to school. Louise had loaned her a book about abstract art, which reminded Jean how she missed the routine of studying. And Midge—maybe Jean could find a way to talk to her about what had happened with Cathy and Cracker. Midge would understand in a way Carmen never could. As she turned over in bed, struggling for a comfortable position on the hard mattress, the old images came to her, Cracker, rolling on the ground whinnying in pain; Cathy, her blond hair tousled around her face, her cornflower blue eyes filled with horror. Resolutely Jean summoned up an image of Chopper, so different from Cracker but with the same affectionate personality. Tomorrow she'd manage to break through Midge's caution.

But Midge was all business the next morning, working Chopper in the ring until Jean protested. "Midge, I think Chopper needs a little more time and patience . . ."

"I know, Jean, but I'm scheduled to go back on patrol tomorrow. Chopper will be fine, don't you worry."

But Jean did worry, as she saw the nervous way Chopper

tossed his head when they trotted past one of the hurdles. She hoped Midge was right.

When it was time for lunch, Midge went for sandwiches, beef brisket, "the best in town," Midge said. Chopper was quietly munching hay in his stall, and even Midge relaxed as she looked out at the Manhattan skyline, chewing her beef brisket.

"This is nice, isn't it?" she asked Jean with a smile.

"It sure is," said Jean. She took a deep breath. "Say, Midge, I wanted to talk to you—" But before she could finish her sentence, an older man in a uniform approached them.

"O'Brien," he barked without preamble. "How's the ankle?"

"All healed up, Captain," said Midge, jumping to her feet.

"Good," said the man. "Because we're shorthanded tonight. We have to use everyone." He gestured at Jean. "This the new groom you were telling me about?"

"Yes sir."

"Hmmmm." His eyes swept Jean from head to toe, taking in the D.A., the grimy white T-shirt, the jeans with the long keychain, the scuffed black oxfords. Without another word he turned and walked away.

Jean watched him go, indignation and fear churning inside her. "It's a good thing this is temporary," she finally said.

"Oh, don't let the captain get to you," Midge said apologetically. "He's always like that, but he's really a good guy." Without pausing she continued, "You know, I've been meaning to talk to you, Jean, about your appearance." Midge kept her eyes on her sandwich. "You'd probably get along better in this world if you changed your hairstyle a little bit—you know, to something more feminine—and got rid of that keychain—"

Jean thought about little Lester Brown back in Doylestown who never grew to be more than four feet tall, and how it sometimes made folks uncomfortable to be around him until they got used to his looking a little different. But nobody ever asked him to wear platform shoes, or walk around on stilts, pretending to be tall. She crumpled the sandwich wrappings wordlessly. First it would just be changing her hair or her clothes, then it would be pretending to laugh when the policemen made jokes about "queers."

Just then, Jean spotted an attractive woman in her early thirties coming up behind Midge. Jean took in green eyes which matched the woman's tailored skirt and jacket, and rich brown hair in a smart gamine style. As Jean watched, the woman put both hands over Midge's eyes. "Guess who!" she sang out, the smile on her face leaving little doubt as to her feelings for Midge.

"Tilly!" Midge's face relaxed into a smile, but the next moment it clouded over again. "You know it's not a good idea to come to the stables." Suddenly remembering Jean, she added nervously, "This is my roommate, Tilly. She's . . . she's allergic to horses. That's why it's a bad idea for her to come around here."

Tilly extended her hand with a smile. "You must be Jean. Midge has talked about you a lot."

Jean shook Tilly's hand, then quickly made her excuses and left. She laughed bitterly at the feelings she'd had for Midge, at her thoughts of confiding in Midge. Midge, ashamed of a woman like Tilly, who clearly loved her so much. Jean knew now that she would get no help from Midge.

That evening, she kept brooding about Midge and Tilly, and Chopper. She knew she should leave the job at the stables, but she couldn't bear to abandon Chopper. She'd thought she was through with horses, through with hope and love, but he'd made her realize she wasn't. Usually, Jean would tuck into the heaping plates of pasta that Luigi generously provided, always insisting that they were included in the price of the room, and she wouldn't stop until she'd soaked up every last bit of sauce with thick slices of Italian bread. Tonight she just pushed the pasta around on her plate. Luigi paused by her table, his plump cheeks sagging in exaggerated dismay.

"Whatsa matta, Jean? I make your favorite meatballs and you don't even touch them!"

Jean tried to smile. "I'm sorry, Luigi, the food's tip-top like always. I've had something weighing on my mind all day and now I guess it's decided to weigh on my stomach for a while."

"What is it, Jean? A fella? You kids always think every little thing is the end of the world."

Jean couldn't help a wry smile as she reassured Luigi, "It's nothing, I'm sure I'll be fine tomorrow." Glancing at the clock over the counter, she pushed her plate away from her and got up. It was time to head over to the Stonewall.

Over at the bar it seemed like everybody was in a somber mood. "Who died?" Jean asked Carmen sardonically, but the big drag queen didn't laugh. "Today was the service for Judy," she responded heavily. She left Jean standing there, regretting her quick tongue, and went over to the jukebox. The strains of "The Man That Got Away" filled the room.

"Jean, bring up a coupla kegs from downstairs," Tony shouted at her.

"You got it, Tony."

When Jean had brought up the kegs, Stony, one of the women who was a regular at the bar, beckoned her over. "Say, kid, you better be on your toes tonight," she advised Jean.

"Thanks, Stony—I will be. Trouble in the air, huh?"

"Yeah," Stony sighed. "You know, kid, I wish I could say I remembered a time when I could sit and have a drink and not feel like trouble was breathing down my neck."

Jean nodded sadly, and bought Stony a beer before she took up her position by the door.

It was with a sense of resignation, that she saw the police car pull up to the curb sometime after midnight. "Betty Law!" she cried, flicking the lights. The drag queens dancing together in the main bar separated. The go-go boy scrambled down from his gilded cage. Everywhere there were cries of "Oh please!" and "Not again." Jean quickly snatched a beer and sat at a table, pretending to be a customer. Sullenly she showed her ID to the uniformed detective who came in the door. Tonight she didn't care if she was arrested. "You a boy or a girl?" the officer smirked. "You got on three pieces of woman's clothing? You ever had a real man?" But his attention was pulled away by Carmen, who was trying to slip by carrying a cigar box full of cash. "I'll take that off your hands, 'lady,' " he said. And Jean took the opportunity to slip out the door.

Outside she was surprised to see that the street and the little park across the way were filling up with people—neighbors, patrons from the folk bar down the street, Stonewall regulars who'd escaped arrest. She stood there too, watching, waiting for something to happen.

The police were herding the most flamboyant drag queens into the paddy wagon when it started. Jean saw one of the policemen push Carmen, so that she tripped in her high heels and fell hard on the pavement. "Pigs!" someone in the crowd shouted. The police pushed another of the drag queens, and she pushed back. The crowd roared its approval, and now they were throwing things, and everyone was scuffling. Some of the queens were freeing themselves from the paddy wagon. Jean heard the sound of a gun, a warning shot, and suddenly she was back in the hollow.

She was kissing Cathy's face, feeling her softness, feeling Cathy's hands on her. They were half sitting, half lying next to Cracker, who was cropping grass peacefully. The steady munching blended in with the trembling of their bodies as they pressed up against each other. It was the first time, for both of them . . .

And then there was the shot, and Cracker had fallen, whinnying with pain, and there was Cathy's father standing with a rifle in his hand, a look of hate on his face. "I missed," was all he said. Cathy was sobbing hysterically, her hands shaking as she buttoned her blouse. She had offered no resistance when her father took her arm and led her to the car up on the road. And Jean had been left with Cracker, watching the blood pump out of the big vein on his neck, watching his eyes glaze over as death took him . . .

The terrified whinnying echoed again in Jean's head, and then she was back in Sheridan Square and she realized it wasn't an echo, it was real. A troop of police horses was advancing on the rioters, and there was Midge struggling to control Chopper, who had broken ranks, whinnying in fear.

Jean ran over and grabbed Chopper's bridle. "Midge, what are you doing? Don't you see what this is doing to Chopper?"

"Jean!" Midge gasped. "What are you doing here?"

"This is where I live, Midge, these are my people. Don't tell me you haven't guessed that! What are *you* doing here?"

"I'm upholding the law," Midge shot back. She took a deep breath. "Jean—I know it's hard to understand—"

"What does Tilly think of you 'upholding the law'?" Jean asked. Midge stiffened and Jean knew that her dig had hit home.

"Tilly understands!" Midge shot back, "Why can't you? Is all this"—she gestured at the line of drag queens mocking the police with high kicks—"worth risking jail for?"

"Yes!" shouted Jean, just as one of the drag queens was torn from the line by a policeman with billy club raised.

Then a shout came from a retreating policeman in riot gear, "O'Brien! Get over here! Now!"

"Let go of my horse," said Midge harshly.

"I won't!" Jean cried. "Stop trying to make Chopper into something he isn't, something he can't be! When will you learn? When will you ever learn?"

Just then, a rock flew from the crowd, hitting Chopper on his scarred legs. With a frightened whinny he reared, tossing Midge from the saddle. Jean tried to hang on, but the frantic horse was too much for her, and the next thing she knew the reins were yanked from her hands and she heard the distant sound of hoofbeats fading away down Christopher Street.

A few nights later, Jean walked into the Colony and looked around. On the surface, everything seemed the same—Dorothy, Marcie, the sad-eyed girl at the bar—but somehow, everything had changed. Dorothy and Frankie were sitting with Marcie and a long-haired man folding leaflets. The sad-eyed girl at the bar didn't look so sad, and was in earnest discussion with a sharp-featured girl with black hair. The jukebox wasn't playing "So Long," but some new song about "Respect." Only the drunk at the back table, her head lying in a pool of beer, looked like the old days.

The bartender waved Jean over. "Could you give me a hand with that drunk in the back? These people are going to hold a meeting here."

"Sure," said Jean. She went to the back table and pulled the drunk into a sitting position, then started back in horror. "Midge!" she exclaimed.

Midge's head flopped forward. "Tilly . . . Jean . . . Chopper . . . nobody understands li'l Midge," she muttered thickly. "N'body cares 'bout my sac'fices . . . did th' best I could . . ." She trailed off and collapsed on the table again.

"You know her?" said the bartender. "There someone we can call?"

"Yes," choked out Jean. "I'll take care of it." She used the bar phone to call Tilly. "Midge is here at the Colony," she explained tersely. "She's too drunk to walk."

After several more unsuccessful attempts to rouse Midge, a cab pulled up and Tilly leaped out. "Oh Midge," she mourned. "I was afraid of something like this." Turning to Jean, she said, "Thank you, Jean, and try to understand. Midge's problem is overidentification with her father, which compelled her to embrace a patriarchal power system, while her own desires placed her squarely in opposition to that very system. She does the best she can."

Jean nodded slowly. "I guess I do understand, a little bit. And maybe I could forgive her, if it wasn't for Chopper."

"Chopper!" Midge echoed drunkenly, tears streaming down her freckled face. "Best horse I ever had, 'cept for Lucky. Lucky dead, Chopper dead, all dead . . ."

Jean's blood froze. Chopper was—dead?

Tilly spoke, in answer to Jean's unspoken question. "We don't know what happened to Chopper. Midge hasn't seen him since that night."

Jean collapsed into a chair, her face in her hands. When she looked up again, there was a large frame blocking the doorway. Could it be? Jean wiped the tears from her eyes and looked again. A familiar whinny told her that she wasn't seeing things. Chopper! "Midge!" she cried, hugging the drunken woman. "Look who's here!"

"Hey, Jean, I've been looking for you!" Louise said with her wide smile as she squeezed past Chopper. "I thought maybe you'd have an idea of what I could do with this horse I found. Do you know him? I was keeping him at my friend Andy's place, the Factory, but they're getting into psychedelics right now, and it didn't seem like the best environment for a horse. What do you think? Should I take him to my parents' place in the Hamptons? They run a dressage school."

"Chopper!" Jean flung her arms around the horse. "I think Chopper would love the Hamptons!"

"Poor li'l Midge never got t'go t'th' Hamptons," Midge muttered.

The long-haired man approached the group by the door. "We're having a meeting here in a little while," he said, distributing fliers. "Maybe some of you would be interested in coming." Jean looked at the flier, which announced at the top "The Gay Liberation Front." Liberation—that had a sweet sound.

"I'm certainly interested," Tilly declared, folding the flier up and putting it in her pocketbook. "After Midge has had a little coffee, we'll both be back! It's time some changes were made."

"Sounds fabulous," Louise agreed. "Can Chopper stay?"

"Liberation is for everyone," the man answered earnestly.

As Chopper drank from a bucket by the bar, and Midge and Tilly got into their cab, Jean stood in the doorway, surveying the Village. Times sure were changing. "Here," said the sharp-featured dark-haired girl, thrusting a pamphlet into her hands. *"SCUM Manifesto,"* Jean read out loud. She looked after the woman, who was hurrying down the street, rudely jostling a young woman who approached the Colony timidly. The young woman paused in the shadow of the building, and Jean noticed that she carried a small suitcase. "Excuse me," she said to Jean. "Can you tell me which way Greenwich Village is?"

Jean smiled. The young woman reminded her of herself, when she had arrived in town, little more than a week ago.

"I—I'm a little lost," the woman continued nervously.

That voice. It was jogging something in Jean's memory. A voice she thought she'd never hear again. Then the woman stepped closer, looking more closely at Jean, and the light of the doorway fell on her beaming face. "You're not lost anymore, Cathy," Jean cried happily as she gathered the beautiful blond girl into her arms. The two girls embraced tightly as the moon shone down on the gathering throngs of proud gay people.

Miss Barnard's Unit

Pauline Peel's heart pounded as the train pulled into Victoria Station. She peered through her compartment window at the throngs of people hurrying to and fro. There were uniformed porters, women up for a day of shopping, men from the City in their silk bowlers, but most of all soldiers—soldiers of every rank and from every branch of service, having tea at the Lyons corner house, saying goodbye to their sweethearts and mothers, some even sleeping, their heads pillowed on their kit bags, as they waited for the trains that would take them to the boats that awaited them in the harbor, and from there to the front.

"And soon I'll be there too!" Pauline thought to herself. Her eyes glowed with excitement in her thin face as she thought about the field hospital where she would soon be stationed, the ambulances, the wounded soldiers—the work that would give her a new purpose in life. For a moment, she caught sight of her reflection in the train window. Her face wasn't what one would call pretty, that

Pauline knew. But it was a face that promised forthrightness and loyalty, and perhaps, if stirred by the right person, even passion. Yes, Pauline decided, it was a good face.

"Excuse me, if you please," a haughty voice interrupted her reverie. The train had come to a stop and the others in her compartment were waiting to get off. A girl with her golden curls modishly dressed under a small hat pushed past her and twitched the compartment door open. Pauline had noticed the girl when she boarded the train at Rotherhithe. She was about Pauline's age, but otherwise the two were complete opposites. This girl was dressed in the height of fashion, her skirt several daring inches above her ankles, while Pauline's tweeds looked dowdy and countrified. Then there was the girl's bored, discontented expression, while Pauline gazed at everyone about her with eager friendliness.

"I'm glad I'm not her," thought Pauline as the golden-haired girl disappeared from view. The girl was probably a society debutante, attending parties and dances while the fate of Europe was being decided.

"Take your bags, miss?" A porter paused beside her.

"No—but can you tell me where I might find the Englishwomen's Volunteer Unit attached to the French Army?"

"Round the corner, beside the sweetshop, miss," said the porter, pointing. "Are you an ambulance driver then?" he called after her as she hurried away, and Pauline replied over her shoulder, "I hope to be!"

She felt bewildered and a little lost as she pushed her way through the crowd, her eyes searching for the Englishwomen Volunteers. She had been to London only twice before, both times with her father, Paul Peel. But Mr. Peel was headmaster of St. Bart's, and could not leave the school during the end-of-term match. "Sometimes I think the fate of Europe will be decided on the playing fields of England," he had told her solemnly before she departed. "And I must do my little all to prepare these boys."

Pauline knew that her father secretly wished she were a boy, someone who could lead men into battle, and she felt his disappointment keenly. Her mother had perished while bringing Pauline into the world, and there had been no feminine presence to counter her father's virile influence. Pauline had been raised at St. Bart's, playing rugger and football with her father's students as if she were one of the lads, and it had come as a great shock to realize that this war was a game from which she was excluded.

She had been in a black despair until her old governess had written to her about the Englishwomen's Volunteer Unit. "They need girls like you," she had written, "strong girls, courageous girls, girls who can tend to soldiers without any romantic nonsense." And Pauline had felt a stirring inside her. "Yes, I can be useful, woman though I am! Even because of the kind of woman I am—a woman not like other women. But how not like other women—what kind of woman am I? Will I meet other women like me, who can tell me what kind of woman I am? Or will it be a woman unlike myself, who will show me what kind of woman I can be?"

As if in answer to her thoughts, the crowd suddenly parted to reveal a tall, handsome woman, the kind of woman, Pauline suddenly realized, that she had always wanted to meet, without even knowing that such a woman existed. Her severely handsome face, under a cap of close-cropped graying hair, was made even more attractive by her air of decision and authority. Pauline caught her breath as she saw that the woman wore the uniform and insignia of the Englishwomen's Volunteer Ambulance

Corps, with braid on her arm that marked her as a captain.

"Soon I'll have a uniform like that!" thought Pauline rapturously. She had always wanted a uniform. Timidly, she addressed the dazzling figure. "I—I'm Pauline Peel," she said.

The older woman smiled, and her craggy face gleamed with warmth. "Yes, Miss Peel, I've been expecting you." Her eyes traveled over the gangly young girl before her. "What is your age, Miss Peel?" she asked.

"I'm nineteen," said Pauline, all at once terribly conscious of her youth and inexperience. A pained expression flitted across the woman's face. "So young . . . so young," she murmured. Then her mood changed abruptly, and she said crisply, "I'm Miss Barnard. I'll be your field commander. Follow me, please."

Pauline hurried after Miss Barnard, who threaded her way swiftly through the crowd. She followed her down a dim passageway, across a street, and then they were among the baggage cars. "Have you got Emma, Joe?" cried Miss Barnard. "Yes, miss, right and tight," called back a wizened little man. Then to Pauline's great shock, she saw not another recruit like herself, but a beautiful chestnut hunter, tail clubbed and mane braided, clip-clopping down the baggage ramp. The weary look seemed to vanish from Miss Barnard's face as she stroked the splendid animal's forelock, and crooned to her, "Don't worry, Emma, we won't be separated anymore."

The rest of the day was a whirl of activity, as Pauline was outfitted for her uniform and instructed in the use of her gas mask. She was introduced to her fellow recruits, a very merry bunch. Pauline, who wasn't much used to the company of other girls, was surprised to find this group so congenial until one of them explained, "Did your governess recommend you too? We all came specially recommended by our governesses. My governess and Miss Barnard were at school together." "Why so was mine!" "Mine too!" chimed in the other girls. "High command gave Miss Barnard her pick of the volunteers after she got the Croix de Guerre," one girl remarked knowingly.

Pauline especially liked her new roommate, Valérie Burne-Jones, a lively girl with black hair and snapping black eyes, whose accent and way of exclaiming "*Nom de dieu!*" were explained by the fact that she was half-French. She told Pauline many interesting things about their commander. Miss Barnard had been at the front for more than a year and had won several medals for bravery, when the shelling of a field hospital had resulted in the death of a particular protégée of hers. After that, Miss Barnard had returned to England. "Pneumonia, they say, but I hear other things," confided Valérie, pointing to her head. "I hear it was, how you say, the shell shock." There was some talk of giving her an administrative post in London, but Miss Barnard had insisted on returning to the front.

"She is more useful at the front," Valérie declared. "For her girls would follow her anywhere! *Nom de dieu,* I feel the same way, and I have only known her two hours!"

"I feel the same way too!" said Pauline eagerly.

"I think maybe this *cheval,* this Emma, is so Miss Barnard should not feel too friendless," Valérie continued thoughtfully. "Some people say it is mad, to take a pet horse to the front. Me, I like horses."

"Yes," Pauline agreed without much conviction, "I suppose I do too." Pauline wanted to like horses, indeed felt somehow that she *should* like horses, but her few attempts at riding had been unsuccessful. And yet, when she thought of Miss Barnard's ecstatic face as she embraced Emma, she felt a renewed desire to understand this special relationship between woman and horse.

Their conversation was interrupted by a knock on the door, followed by Miss Barnard's entrance. "Girls, I want you to meet another recruit, Miss Flora Thurlow," she said without preamble. "Quarters are tight, so Miss Thurlow will bed down with you. We must make the best of things in wartime."

"Yes, Miss Barnard," said Valérie, but Pauline was not thinking about the cramped quarters. She was staring in amazement at the newcomer, who was none other than the fashionable girl from the train!

She had not lost her haughty air, and Valérie was the first to speak after the door had closed behind Miss Barnard. "Pauline and I can share a bed," she said kindly, for there were only two beds in the room. "We are friends already, yes?" She turned to Pauline with a smile. "Yes, yes, of course," Pauline replied absently. Flora Thurlow did not acknowledge the gesture. She merely put her overnight case on the bed closest to the window and said, "I shall sleep here."

Long after Valérie had fallen asleep, Pauline lay awake thinking of Miss Barnard, her father, the end-of-term match, and Flora Thurlow. What impulse had moved this high-bred girl to join the volunteers? From the gossip they'd heard at supper, it was clear that Miss Thurlow was more accustomed to luncheons with Mrs. Hythe-Jenkyns, or balls at Lady Bellamy's, than the rigors of war.

When Pauline had nearly exhausted her ponderings and was close to sleep, the subject of her thoughts suddenly sat up in bed and looked cautiously about. Taking some writing implements from her overnight case, Flora crept to a seat by the window and, illuminated only by the full moon, she began to write with an intensity almost frightening. After she had covered several sheets of monogrammed notepaper, she stopped and looked up. The bright moonlight revealed a face marked with tears and anguish. After a moment or two, Flora covered her face with her hands and Pauline could only just make out the words that Flora uttered in a low voice, "Why, why do I do this? I *must* stop and I will, yes, I *will* stop." Just then, Valérie stirred in her sleep, and muttered, *"Plus bas, ma cherie."* Glancing fearfully toward the two girls, Flora hastily climbed back into her own bed.

Pauline's curiosity was piqued by the strange behavior of this intriguing girl, and the next morning she couldn't restrain herself from glancing into Flora's open overnight case, while the other girl was washing up. Beneath a dainty chambray shirtwaist, the corner of a letter peeked out, and just before Flora reentered the room, Pauline was able to see that it was addressed to Berlin.

"The WC is free now," she told Pauline curtly as she put away her toiletries and snapped her overnight case shut. "Th-thank you," stammered Pauline as she fled to the WC, her thoughts in a whirl of curiosity and bewilderment. Was that the letter so strangely and secretly written the night before? Who could Flora possibly be writing to in Berlin? What was the meaning of her strange self-recriminations? Suspicion darkened her thoughts, but Pauline bade herself not to judge too hastily, for in these times of war, nothing was what it seemed. It was as if the old safe world had been somehow inverted to create a strange, yet exciting new world. Even Pauline herself was part of this inversion—why, a week ago she would never have dreamed of prying into another girl's belongings. And the oddest thing was, despite her own half-formed suspicions, and the other girl's cold reserve, she found herself strangely drawn to Flora!

The next morning, as the unit made their way aboard ship, Pauline forgot about her mysterious roommate as she was again caught up in the excitement of going to the front. Nor was she alone. Each member of the unit seemed positively feverish with anticipation. "Soon we'll be part of the big show!" burst out a girl called Georgina Smythe. She turned to Flora, who happened to be standing beside her along the ship's rail. "Won't it be awfully jolly?"

"It isn't the word I should use," remarked Flora acidly. "War means a bit more than a day spent following the hounds and then tea by the fire." The only time Flora showed any emotion was when Miss Barnard led Emma aboard. Then her eyes sparkled with a sudden animation. "Another horse lover," thought Pauline to herself. How strange that two people so different as Miss Barnard and Flora Thurlow shared the same attraction to horses.

Later, when most of the girls, even the stalwart Miss Barnard, were confined to their cabins with seasickness, Pauline found Flora at Emma's stall, quietly soothing the horse as the boat plunged up and down.

"How good you are with her!" exclaimed Pauline admiringly. "I shouldn't know what to do. I haven't been around horses very much, and now I'm starting to wonder if I haven't missed something rather special."

Flora's hauteur relaxed a trifle. "I should say you have. Here." She put her hand in her coat pocket. "Would you like to give her a lump of sugar? I saved it from my tea."

Gingerly, Pauline offered Emma the sugar cube, her hand held out flat, palm up, as Flora had shown her. She felt Emma's gentle, hairy lips moving over her hand, and she closed her eyes, to better savor the indescribable sensation. When she opened them, her hand was empty and Emma was crunching the sugar between her strong jaws. Pauline looked up to find Flora's violet eyes regarding her knowingly.

"You begin to see, don't you?" said Flora.

Before they debarked at Calais, Miss Barnard gathered the volunteers by Emma's stall. She spoke briefly, but forcefully, of the work that lay ahead of them, ending, "Remember, girls—Rule Britannia!" Pauline thrilled through at Miss Barnard's words, and when she stole a quick glance at Flora, she saw that, though her face was averted, her bosom rose and fell with emotion.

The weeks that followed were busier than Pauline could have imagined. The work was hard, as Miss Barnard had promised, and unrelenting. No sooner would the unit have succeeded in safely transporting a sea of wounded soldiers, left in the wake of battle, from the front to the field hospital, than the call would come that there had been more fighting and once again they would set about their grim task. Sometimes, Pauline would come across a wounded German soldier on the field, but she knew, much as it pained her, that it was all the overtasked unit could do to help their own. Still, she could not help thinking that groans of pain sounded the same in any language. In the midst of all that Pauline saw, she soon forgot about Flora's German correspondence—her earlier suspicions now seemed like some child's game, dreamed up for amusement when there had been time for such things.

In the rare quiet moments, Pauline enjoyed the gay companionship of the other girls and, whenever possible, that of Flora. Flora, however, was not popular with the rest of the unit. The girls found her habitual haughtiness off-putting, and were vexed by her imperious demands for a solitary berth, for the rest of the unit cheerfully doubled up, owing to a chronic bed shortage. Valérie, who was as popular as Flora was disliked, would sometimes sleep three-a-bed with two of her special chums. Even Miss Barnard, who could have easily demanded privacy as just compensation for the rigors of command, shared her bed with Millicent, one of the new recruits, who was said to bear a striking resemblance to Miss Barnard's dead protégée.

Yet with Pauline, Flora was almost friendly at times, particularly when they met for a quick chat in Emma's stall. Flora was eager to share her horsemanship with Pauline, and the result was that Pauline had become terribly fond of Emma. Yet her early riding failures were still vivid in her memory, and whenever Flora suggested they ride, Pauline would find some excuse to refuse. Her cowardice shamed her, for it seemed that everyone in the unit was at least a competent rider and Valérie had entertained them all with some trick riding she'd picked up from "*une amie de la cirque.*"

Whatever petty squabbles might divide the girls, they all shared a concern for their beloved leader. The girls had soon realized that Miss Barnard was not fully recovered from her illness, which seemed to have little to do with pneumonia. In times of crisis, no one could be more relied upon than their stern-faced commander, yet in those few quiet moments when the need for discipline was relaxed, and the unit could rest and daydream, Miss Barnard's behavior would grow increasingly queer.

It was during one of these spells that the superintendent from London paid a visit. The girls were frantic with

Flora put a comforting arm around Pauline. "But uline, what happened?"

"Oh, Flora! I've only ridden sidesaddle and both times was a perfect disaster! I simply couldn't stay on the rse, much as I tried. The horse was made perfectly misable and I looked a fool," sniffled Pauline.

"Oh, silly Pauline," laughed Flora, with more gaiety an Pauline had yet seen her display. "A woman like you s never meant to ride sidesaddle. Put on these trousers d get on that horse. You will ride astride, and unless I 1 quite mistaken, you will like it."

Pauline was doubtful, but determined to try this thing, for no other reason than to preserve her newfound closess with Flora, a closeness Pauline had been yearning for, nost since first they had met. Once Pauline, now jauntily ired in the trousers, had mounted the waiting animal, e knew of an instant that Flora's judgment had been und. Pauline had never been the problem, nor had the rse been at fault. It was only convention, convention d custom and tradition, all the things so highly prized those who made up society and formed its judgments, at had kept Pauline from riding, that which was so natal an occupation for a woman such as she.

As Pauline rode, she felt a surge of power and excitent, discovering for herself at last that feeling which ew those such as Flora and Miss Barnard to the saddle. s it to be a horse," Pauline pondered, "rather than a oman, who is to be the key to my discovery of myself as woman?" Yet Pauline could not forget that it was none her than a woman who had led her to this horse, and at woman was Flora. And then the ride was over, Emma s cooled and groomed and bedded, and there were only uline and Flora.

worry. If the superintendent were to see M her current state, she would surely be England, yet they could not imagine continu without the special guidance and understa captain. Much to everyone's surprise and stepped in and distracted the snobbish wom ety gossip while the other girls hastily Barnard out of sight.

Pauline glowed with pride at Flora's quick Georgina spoke for all the girls when she heartily on the shoulder, crying, "Jolly go egg!" Flora thawed to a distant friendliness u warmth, and only the hot-tempered Valérie the society girl. "Pauline, *ma chérie,* you k *tendre*, an affection for you, as I have for all worry. I do not understand how you can be by that *princesse de neige*, that how you say, A girl like that, I would not trust." Even as Pa off the French girl's dramatic warning, she th first time in weeks, of the mysterious letter to

Shortly after the superintendent's visit, ord for the unit to move still closer to the front. before they were to pull out, Flora invited P her in a visit to Emma. Pauline was only t chance to spend time with the two, but w when she arrived at the old barn to find that ready saddled up the hunter and was thrust trousers at Pauline.

"It will be too dangerous for riding once w to the front. This may be your last chance with a bluntness born of wartime.

"But Flora," Pauline pleaded, "I simply ca and . . . and . . . oh, it's just too horrible to talk

"I have never seen one take to the saddle so naturally as you," Flora said.

Pauline blushed at the compliment, but Flora was not yet done. In an awed tone she added, "Why, Pauline, nearly all of the girls in the unit are experienced horsewomen, yet I would wager that none has a better seat than you."

Pauline marveled that the intimacy she had longed for from Flora was now at hand. If only she had dared to mount Emma from the first! Pauline silently cursed society, for its unnatural restraints on the relationship between woman and horse.

That night Flora joined gaily in the suppertime chatter, and as the girls straggled off to bed, yawning, she put a hand on Pauline's arm and said almost shyly, "Won't you come to my room? I want to tell you more about the hunt at Rotherhithe."

Flora and Pauline arose later than the others the next morning, and came downstairs to a scene of bedlam. They were to pull out in less than an hour, yet no one could find Miss Barnard, and leadership was forthcoming from no other quarter. Pauline immediately set the girls about packing rolls of bandages, cases of foie gras, and other necessities, while Flora made straight for the barn. By the time the unit was ready to leave, Flora had returned with Miss Barnard, and no reference was made to her strange absence.

Later, Flora confided to Pauline that she had found their commander in the barn, trying to saddle up Emma. When Flora had pulled the saddle away from her, Miss Barnard began to call for Mary, her dead protégée, and babble that she didn't want to do her embroidery or French, that Nurse had said she could go riding. Flora had pleaded with her, barked orders at her, and finally, in a fit of desperation, delivered a bracing slap to Miss Barnard's cheek. This final measure had brought the older woman back to herself.

The girls had scarcely settled into their new quarters, a small French farmhouse, which might have seemed quite charming under happier circumstances, when the call to duty came from headquarters. Pauline and Flora were sent out in different vehicles and twice that day Pauline nearly drove her ambulance into a ditch, so distracted was she by thoughts of Flora. Finally, as dusk was falling, Pauline gathered up her last load of wounded.

For a moment, before starting back to the field hospital, Pauline surveyed the stark landscape of the battlefield. As the shadows lengthened and enveloped the once fertile field, Pauline felt as if she were witness to death itself on its inexorable march across Europe. Pauline was about to start the motor when she noticed two figures in the distance, nearly hidden in the shadows. It was Flora, some hundred yards off, tending to a fallen soldier on the field.

"I won't be a moment, lads," Pauline reassured the groaning soldiers as she jumped out of the auto and hurried across the field. Flora's name was on her lips when Pauline pulled up short. Flora was conversing with the soldier in rapid German! Instinctively, Pauline shrank behind a shattered tree, watching and listening in astonishment as Flora carried on an urgent conversation with the wounded Hun, then gave him bandages and a small amount of whiskey. Pauline's mind was in a whirl. Keeping herself concealed from Flora, she crept back to the waiting men.

Once back in the ambulance, even the moans of the wounded could not drown out Pauline's thoughts as she drove automatically to the hospital. Yes, Pauline herself had felt sympathy for those young boys whom the men who sat in comfortable rooms far from the front had labeled her enemy, but she could not think it right to give away items that were in such short supply. And was there some connection between the urgent conversation Pauline had just witnessed and Flora's troubling letter to Berlin? Pauline resolved that she would have it out with Flora that night.

Flora had gone to bed when Pauline arrived at the farmhouse. Pauline hurried up the stairs, and knocked timidly at her door. "Flora? It is I—Pauline. May I come in?" she queried anxiously. A muffled voice responded, "I'm sorry, Pauline, I have a terrible headache. I must rest." Unhappily Pauline went downstairs to join the rest of the girls around the supper table. The voice had sounded like the old Flora—cold and reserved. Pauline's friends watched her sympathetically as she picked at her coq au vin without appetite.

After the meal was over, Valérie took her hand and urged gently, "*Viens, ma chérie,* tonight you will sleep with me."

But Pauline only shook her head. "Thank you, Valérie, you're very kind," she said, summoning a brave smile, "but tonight I somehow feel I must be alone."

Pauline hurried away to sleep in Emma's stall, while Valérie's expression darkened. "*Cette princesse de neige doit être punie!*" she spit out, and the other girls agreed with her, although they didn't understand her.

Thus when Flora came downstairs the next morning, she found herself surrounded on all sides by unmistakable hostility. For her part, Flora immediately resumed her haughty air. Pauline longed to speak to the other girl, and it seemed to her that as they headed out the door, Flora hesitated a moment, and would have waited for Pauline, but Valérie quickly linked her arm through Pauline's and gestured toward Flora as she spoke with mocking politeness, "*Après vous!*"

But now, the battle of Compiègne raged and the wounded piled up all around them and that was all that there was. Who should share a bed with whom was of no importance when there was to be sleep for none. Flora worked beside the other girls, and none could have faulted her dedication. As for Miss Barnard, as was her nature, when the work was hardest and danger closest at hand, she was at her finest. Miss Barnard remained splendidly calm, maintaining radio contact with the front and sending the ambulances back and forth between the field hospitals and the battlefield. And when Millicent collapsed in nervous exhaustion at the end of the third day, Miss Barnard turned the radio over to one of the less severely injured officers and drove an ambulance herself until the last wounded soldier had been taken away.

Afterward, when it was no longer necessary for Miss Barnard to command, the girls once again found her in the barn, with Emma. This time, she spoke directly to the horse in a manner which left the girls aghast. "Dearest Mary," Miss Barnard said softly, "you've come back. It is so good to see you. You cannot know how pleased I am to find that I did not kill you. Now we can be together always, as I promised we would be." At this last, Miss Barnard moved closer to the puzzled horse, lips trembling, but before anything further could transpire, several of the girls grabbed hold of Miss Barnard and pulled her back.

Millicent gently led their babbling commander away, while Mabel, who'd been with the unit from the first, related to the others what had become of Mary. The unit had all been gathered at the field hospital when word arrived that a skirmish had broken out and they must set out at once for the volatile area. Miss Barnard had insisted that Mary stay in the relative safety of the hospital, while the others returned to the front. No one could have predicted that a stray mortar would hit the hospital, and that Mary would be the unit's only casualty that day. Shortly after that, Miss Barnard had returned to England to recover from "pneumonia."

Much might have been made of this by the girls, who were prone to gossip and speculation, but after three days and nights of tireless labor, sleep soon claimed all, even, mercifully, Miss Barnard. No call for their services came that next day, and so, for the first time in nearly a fortnight, the unit had no other task than that of rest and recovery. Miss Barnard remained in bed, tended to by Millicent, and appeared to be regaining lucidity. Pauline sought out Flora, determined that now they should talk, only to be told by one of the other girls that Flora had slipped out early that morning without a word to anyone.

That evening, the calm of the day gave way to merriment, as the girls gathered around the hearth of the little French farmhouse and passed around a bottle of calvados, along with many ribald remarks. Only Pauline sat apart from the others, gathering courage, for Flora had returned and, without a word to anyone, had gone to one of the upstairs rooms and shut herself in.

"Come on, Mabel, let's go up to bed, do let's," begged Georgina as her roommate grabbed the bottle for another swig. "I won't be henpecked," declared Mabel. But before their quarrel could become serious, Valérie took the bottle from Mabel and, pouring a glass, brought it to Pauline.

"Why so sad, *ma chérie*? Maybe you could let me try to

cheer you up, no? This is something I am very good at, *tu sais*, putting a smile on a woman's face. *Laisse-moi essayer, on peut s'amuser très bien, n'est-ce pas?*"

Pauline hated to refuse Valérie's kindness, but she knew that only Flora could lift this heaviness from her heart. Leaving a resentful Valérie behind, Pauline stole upstairs to Flora's room. This time she didn't knock, only eased the door open a crack, expecting to find Flora in bed. But she had to smother a gasp, for Flora, a tear trickling down her cheek, knelt by the window, grasping an electric torch and slowly flashing it on, off, on, off. Unnoticed, Pauline hurriedly exited.

Pauline had not believed that Flora could be disloyal, yet the evidence was now too great to ignore, and the risk of Pauline's silence too grave. It was common knowledge that this section of the front was weakly defended. Had that been the subject of Flora's discussion with the German soldier, or perhaps the content of some coded message, just now transmitted? Pauline stumbled down the staircase, too distraught to notice where she was going, and suddenly, Valérie was there, holding her and stroking her hair.

"Ah, she has again broken your heart. *Elle est faite de la glace*. But do not worry, Valérie is here."

At these compassionate words from her comrade, Pauline could hold back no longer. She unburdened her heart to Valérie, jumbling together her love of Emma and her feelings for Flora and, finally, relating what she had observed with the letter, the soldier, and the torch. The more she spoke, the angrier Valérie became, and when finally it was Valérie's turn to speak, Pauline was taken aback by her ferocity.

"*Un espion!*" hissed Valérie. "I should have known. Why else would *une femme* such as she have joined the Englishwomen Volunteers? We must go at once to Miss Barnard with this information!"

As much as it pained Pauline, she could not dispute Valérie's decision, and together they made their way to the wing of the house that served as Miss Barnard's headquarters and bedroom. But as they approached her door, there was a tremendous noise and suddenly Pauline and Valérie found themselves on the ground. Screams and chaos erupted all about them.

"A mortar! We've been hit!"

"Is anyone hurt?"

"Where's Miss Barnard?"

As if in response, a scream issued forth from Miss Barnard's room. So chilling was the effect that each woman present stood frozen in place for an awful, helpless moment, before wartime instincts took over. The girls raced to the room and found Miss Barnard standing over Millicent's still body, crying in a harsh, unfamiliar voice, "Not again—not again." With everyone crowded around Millicent, tending feverishly to their fallen comrade, it was some minutes before the girls noticed that Miss Barnard was gone. Agatha was sent out in search of her, and not more than five minutes had passed when the door opened with a bang. Every head turned to see a panic-stricken Agatha stumble in, followed by a gust of icy rain.

"Quick, someone do something! Miss Barnard's having one of her spells and she's riding Emma as fast as ever she can, right towards the front! Oh, it's simply ghastly! Whatever shall we do?"

Now the girls milled about in excitement and distress,

each suggesting a different course of action. "We should have been on the lookout for just this sort of thing," mourned Alice.

"I'll take one of the ambulances," said Mabel, swaying unsteadily to her feet.

"You're drunk!" said Georgina on the verge of tears.

Agatha wrung her hands, wailing, "Emma will be going across the fields, jumping fences. We won't be able to catch her in a motor!"

Where a moment before, Pauline had felt only panic and fright, suddenly she felt clearheaded and purposeful. "There's only one way to catch her, and that's on another horse," said Pauline with decision. "I'll ride Mathieu's carthorse. Quick, Mabel, your trousers." Pauline changed while Valérie saddled up the horse and, with little time lost, Pauline set out in pursuit of Miss Barnard.

When the girls returned from the barn to the house, they found a dazed Flora stumbling down the staircase. Having lost consciousness when hit by a chunk of debris from the blast, she had been oblivious to the excitement downstairs. Forgetting their animosity for Flora, the girls quickly related all that had happened. When they reached the part about Pauline riding after Miss Barnard, Flora turned quite pale.

"Pauline? You say Pauline went after her?" she queried in a voice so fraught with fear as to be almost unrecognizable. "She has only ridden once. Why did you send her? She has ridden but once in her life."

The girls looked at each other, speechless, until finally Alice broke the awful silence. "I assure you, Flora, we had no idea. We should never have let her go if we had. She appeared a most accomplished rider."

"Which way did they go?" Flora asked sharply, shaking

off her despair. "I shall take one of the ambulances and go after them." Flora pulled on her overcoat as she spoke, and was out the door before anyone had a chance to reply. She had just started the motor when Valérie jumped in the other side.

"*Allons-y!* Hurry, we must find them," was all she said. Flora gunned the motor and they were off.

It was a wild night to be abroad, and the blustery winds now covered the moon with clouds, now blew them away so that the countryside was almost as bright as day in the moonlight. Valérie and Flora drove in tense silence, bouncing over the rutted roads. Then Valérie spoke.

"We drive towards the front, but do not be tempted to try any of your dirty business." As she said this, Valérie removed her hand from her pocket to reveal a pistol.

"I must insist that you put that weapon away, Miss Burne-Jones, and you would be well advised to refrain from such wild accusations," Flora replied sharply, never taking her eyes from the road.

Valérie glared at Flora, as if gathering strength for another attack, when they rounded a curve and Flora pointed out the window. "There!" she breathed, and they both saw the unmistakable figure of Emma streaking across the fields and bounding over the rustic fences as if she were running the Grand National, Miss Barnard perfectly balanced in the saddle. "She is like a valkyrie," said Valérie, overcome with admiration, even though it was clear Miss Barnard was quite mad.

"And look!" There was Mathieu's heavy percheron, moving at a lumbering gallop across the fields, his path angled to intercept Miss Barnard's. They could just make out the slim figure clinging to his back, her mac glistening with rain, before a dark cloud covered the moon. "She must have taken, how you call it, a shortcut," Valérie remarked tensely.

"But will she reach her in time?" Flora whispered hoarsely as she gunned the engine and turned into the field. They knew they were very near the front—they could now see the craters made by the recent shelling, and the barbed wire, and hear the distant crack of rifles. Death was very close now. A sudden gust of wind shredded the veil of cloud from the moon, illuminating for an instant the field. Not more than a hundred yards ahead was the form of a thrown rider, struggling to get up, a horse standing nearby with its head hanging down, breathing hard.

Flora stopped the ambulance with a jerk. Flinging herself out of the vehicle, she ran toward the fallen rider with Valérie behind her, squelching rapidly through the mud. When the two reached the fallen figure, they saw it was Pauline trying desperately to lift herself out of the mud. Flora flung her arms around the panting, bedraggled girl. "Oh, Pauline, my Pauline, thank God you're safe," she cried, clutching the sodden head to her bosom.

"Miss Barnard and Emma," was all Pauline managed to get out as she lifted a trembling hand and pointed. Then Flora and Valérie saw it—a few feet away, blending in with the mud and rain and desolation, were two dark mounds which seemed part of the landscape. Flora ran to the prone woman, Valérie at her side and Pauline dragging herself behind. The rain had cleaned the mud from Miss Barnard's face, and they could all see imprinted on it a faintly triumphant smile.

The girls stood a moment in despair, then Valérie wheeled around and pointed accusingly at Flora, *"Tu l'as fait!"* she cried. "You did this thing! You are an *espion,* worse than *les sales boches*!" Even Pauline understood this. The phrase "dirty German" was on everyone's lips these days, no matter the language.

"I am no spy!" said Flora so forcefully, that for a moment Pauline believed her. Then memories of Flora's iniquity rose up like a fresh misery in her mind.

"It's no good, Flora," she shouted through the rising wind. "We know! I saw you signaling with your torch. I saw you speaking with the German yesterday, the letter to Berlin—I could not believe it of you, Flora, but when I saw you with the torch, I knew there could be no other explanation. I can't turn you in . . . just, please . . . go away. Disappear."

"But me, I can turn you in!" said Valérie fiercely. "Or I can deal with you now, like the *chien* you are!" Drawing the pistol from her pocket, Valérie pointed it at Flora. Horrified, Pauline grabbed her arm, and the revolver went off. Flora flinched as the bullet whistled past her ear, and Valérie stood, holding her pistol, looking at it in a sort of shock.

"You fools!" said a low voice. They turned, and to their amazement they saw that Miss Barnard had risen to her full, imposing height. Her eyes flashed with the keen intelligence they remembered, and they knew her sanity had returned at last. "Have you learned nothing from the horrors of war but hate and madness and death?" And as she spoke, Emma, too, struggled to her feet, whinnying a little.

Valérie stood for a moment longer, gazing at her gun. Then, "*Qu'est-ce que j'ai fait?* What have I done?" she wailed, and hurled the gun as far away from her as she could.

"No one has been hurt, this time," said Miss Barnard gently, but with a warning edge. Then she turned toward

Flora and asked slowly, in a level voice, "Miss Thurlow, do you have some explanation to offer?"

"I thought I was in love with Marlene," Flora started, "and she with me." A look of understanding grew on the faces of the other women as they listened.

"We had planned to meet in Switzerland, when I received a letter from her, breaking off our affair. But I could not forget Marlene, and I wrote her again and again, pleading with her to take me back. I knew I would go mad if I continued on in that way, so I joined the Volunteers. The letter I wrote that night was my last and for my benefit alone, for I never posted it."

The look of pain on Pauline's face as Flora spoke of Marlene was unmistakable, and as Flora continued, she moved closer to Pauline, and put an arm around the trembling girl. "Dear Pauline, I did give some few supplies to the German you saw, but no secrets. I knew Klaus from his days as the bouncer at the Kit Kat Klub, where Marlene worked. When I saw him, it was as if the wounds were fresh again and I had to know what had become of her. I learned from him that Marlene had married the owner of the club, an abhorrent little man, but quite well connected—the kind of man who, even in wartime, could procure for Marlene the luxuries she found so indispensable. I must confess this news threw me into a turmoil, and I spent all the next day walking and going over our relationship in my mind. When I returned that night, I went to my room and played a little game that Marlene and I had shared, a child's game of shadow puppets."

"So you were not signaling at all!" Pauline wondered that she could have been so distrustful of actions, which, in retrospect, were clearly quite innocent. But then a darker thought crossed her mind. "So . . . you are still in love with Marlene?"

"No, dear girl, I don't believe I ever was. As I played that child's game, I knew, with certainty, that I was through with Marlene and our childish relationship. I had gone downstairs to tell you just that, when I learned that you had so bravely set off after Miss Barnard." Now Pauline took Flora in her arms, and Flora rested her golden curls on the gangly girl's shoulder.

Then Valérie, who had been uncharacteristically silent throughout Flora's account, spoke at last. "Marlene? Marlene Rauffenstein?"

"Why yes. Are you acquainted with Marlene?" Flora asked with surprise.

"*Oui, cette femme débauchée.* At one time, she broke my heart, and those of many others that I know."

"Broken hearts," sighed Miss Barnard. "War has a way of producing quite a number of those, doesn't it?" Pauline now dared to put an arm around their commander, in her rare moment of weakness, and with typical Gallic warmth, Valérie embraced all three of them.

"Again you are thinking of this Mary, *n'est-ce pas*?" she queried sympathetically.

"Mary, Millicent, all the girls I have lost," replied Miss Barnard.

"Millicent? Why, Millicent will soon be herself again," said Flora with a smile. "She took quite a blow to the head, but when we left the farmhouse, she had already come round."

Pauline felt Miss Barnard stagger, and she would have fallen if Pauline and Valérie had not supported her. "Millicent? Alive?" Miss Barnard choked out. "Can it really be true?" It was agreed that Valérie would drive Miss Barnard back while Flora and Pauline took care of the horses. "And we'll keep this incident to ourselves, girls. No need for the superintendent or the other girls to know," said Miss Barnard firmly.

As she and Flora rode back over the war-torn battlefields, the sun rising behind them, Pauline realized that war was not all uniforms and glory, but also madness, despair, and death. Yet strangely enough, it had brought her a kind of inner quietude, which had taken the place of those questions to which she had so long sought the answers. For Pauline knew now, with a serene sense of inevitability, the kind of woman she was—and glancing at the woman by her side, she marveled that the path she had followed to find herself, had, in the end, led her to Flora.

The Stableboy

Peg rushed in the front door, nearly colliding with her younger brother, Johnny. "Hey sis, where's the fire?" he teased. "Gangway!" Peg panted, pushing past him. Her long legs took the stairs two steps at a time as she raced up to her bedroom on the second floor of their comfortable suburban home. She glanced at the clock on her bedside table, whose hands stood at 3:20. Would she make it? She tore off the crisp white shirt with the Peter Pan collar, the full plaid skirt, the loafers and bobby sox. "Hateful things!" she muttered to herself, tossing them into the back of her closet. Turning, she caught a glimpse of herself in the mirror, her lanky frame clad only in sensible cotton underwear and a tiny "training" brassiere. Peg frowned, disliking the gawky girl she saw, with her bright red hair and freckles. Not quite sixteen, she was unable to appreciate the blossoming sensuality in the full red lips, the keen intelligence shining from candid blue eyes. She saw only the length of her legs, not their shapeliness.

Wasting no time, she pulled on her worn jodhpurs and

an old flannel shirt that had belonged to her beloved Uncle Roger. She tugged on her riding boots, then clumpety-clumped down the back stairs to the kitchen, pulling on her gray wool cardigan. Johnny was taking a Coke from the fridge, balancing his baseball bat, with his mitt slung over it, on his shoulder. He was just taking a noisy gulp when they both heard the front door open and the cool patrician voice of their older sister, Carol. "Peg, are you here? We're going to be late for the meeting of the Fall Frolic decorating committee." In an instant, Peg was out the back door and on her bicycle.

The autumn breeze cooled Peg's flushed cheeks as she rode her bicycle down Meadowbrook Lane toward Chatham Stables. Her heart lightened and the pedals seemed to sing beneath her feet as she got farther away from Carol and the frightening world of femininity she represented, and closer to the stables, her true home. Oh, she'd tried to fit in at Chatham Day School, and at the country club. She'd hunched down to conceal her height. She'd tried to talk about nail polish and Rock Hudson as if she gave a darn about either of them. But deep down Peg knew her efforts were hopeless; she would never be popular—not like Carol, who ruled the smooth set at Chatham Day, Carol with her honey-blond pageboy, and star quarterback Fred Grayson as her steady. At Chatham Day, Peg would always be in the shadow of her older sister. At the stables, she could be herself, surrounded by people who thought horses were the most important thing in the world!

And there was another reason Peg did not want to miss today's visit to the stables: Pat Kowalski, the new stableboy. He was different from other boys, and although she had known him only a week, Peg felt strangely drawn to him. But he was often distant, responding to Peg's questions with clipped monosyllables. To Peg, he was still an enigma.

Here were the stables! Peg glided under the rustic wooden sign and, jumping off her bike, wheeled the vehicle into the tack room. She stood there a moment, inhaling the smells—leather, oats, and that sweaty, musky, indefinable scent that said "horses." Then she went to greet Merrylegs, her faithful old pony. She had belonged to Peg since Peg's ninth birthday, and it seemed not so long ago that she and Merrylegs had been part of a troupe of other little girls and their ponies. Peg sighed. Now the other ponies were sold, their former mistresses no longer interested in horses, instead inexplicably fascinated by clothes and boys. Even Marjorie and Doreen, Peg's closest pals in the pony club days, now acted as if they didn't know a forelock from a fetlock. Peg had heard her mother and Carol discussing her, wondering when she, too, would get past the "horse phase." How desperately Peg wanted them to understand that she would never tire of horses!

As she reached Merrylegs's stall, she heard Pat's voice. "Whisht, girl, whisht," was all he said, in a low soothing tone, and Peg's skin prickled. Deliberately, she sauntered down the line of stalls, trying to act casual.

Pat was in a stall with a beautiful dappled gray mare Peg had never seen before, whose flaring nostrils and fine muzzle revealed thoroughbred blood. She stood no more than sixteen hands, Peg guessed, but every inch of her was marked by perfect conformation. Catching Peg's scent, the new horse put her ears back, and danced away from her, crowding Pat against the wall.

"Whoa!" said Pat, glancing up to see what was alarming the highbred horse. "Watch it," he warned curtly as he caught sight of Peg standing hesitantly in the stall doorway. "Garbo's edgy. She used to be a circus horse, and it seems she was tormented by one of the clowns."

"Oh, how awful," breathed Peg. She stood stock-still as Garbo, her ears back and her eyes rolling, tossed her head up and down rapidly. When Peg didn't move, Garbo calmed down, and finally stretched her neck out to snuffle Peg all over. Peg was like a statue as the beautiful mare tickled her with her whiskers, sending shivers down her spine. She looked deeply into the horse's intelligent brown eyes for a moment, then Garbo dropped her head coyly, and pretended to nibble some hay on the stall floor. In spite of herself, Peg laughed. "What a flirt you are," she crooned, caressing Garbo's velvety nose. The splendid animal accepted the caress, arching her neck with pleasure.

"Well, you've certainly charmed her," Pat observed. "Maybe you can give me a hand here, while I change her dressing."

"I'd love to!" Peg said, still lost in Garbo's rich brown gaze.

Peg held Garbo steady while Pat's skillful fingers unwrapped the bandage from Garbo's right foreleg. From her vantage point, Peg could admire Pat's tanned, muscular forearms and glossy black hair. When the bandage was off, Pat glanced up at Peg, with a swift smile. "The dressing has to be changed every day," he explained. "Garbo has a strained tendon, and the best thing for her is a nice hot pack of Epsom salts." While he worked, he continued talking. "Mrs. Huntley wants to show her when she's well. She's too fine an animal to be just an old saddle horse, teaching little kids how to ride. Mrs. Huntley thinks that by showing her, we could pull in some new business. We're going to try her out on the jumps when she's well."

Together they prepared the new dressing, and soon they were talking away as if they'd known each other forever. Peg told Pat how she'd been coming to the stables since she was six years old, and how much she loved horses. It turned out they'd both read many of the same books—*King of the Wind*, and even *A Girl and Her Horse.*

"How funny that you've read that!" Peg exclaimed. "Most boys won't read something if they think it's a 'girl's book.' "

Pat blushed, and said, "My—my sister had a copy, and I happened to read it when I was sick . . ."

Sensing he was embarrassed, Peg changed the subject. "You're so lucky to have this job here! I'd love to have a job like this, but my mother would never let me. She says, 'There's a reason the term is stable*boy.*' "

"I know," Pat said. "Most places around here wouldn't even think of hiring a stable*girl.*"

"That's awful!" said Peg indignantly. "When I have my own stables, I'm going to hire nobody but girls!" She couldn't help resenting Pat his privileged position, just a little bit.

"I know how you feel," said Pat somberly. "I'm just taking advantage of an outmoded system of discrimination. But I have to." He paused a second and looked at Peg intently with his level gray eyes. "You see . . . we really need the money at home. My Dad died a couple years back, and my mom works as a cleaning lady . . ."

"I—I see," said Peg a little awkwardly, not used to such a frank discussion of finances.

"I haven't told her yet that I'm working here. She wouldn't like the idea of me being a stable . . . boy. She thinks I'm baby-sitting."

"Baby-sitting!" Peg said, surprised.

"Sure," Pat replied, clearing his throat. "Lots of boys baby-sit in Havertown."

Havertown! That was where Della, the Gardner family maid, lived. Peg realized how little she knew about the world outside of Chatham. She was stirred to admiration as she thought of Pat and the hardships he faced. The concerns of the other girls at the country club, her own worries about popularity, and the Fall Frolic suddenly seemed trivial. In a flash, she made up her mind that she would stop trying to fit in. She'd rather be like Pat, making her own way in the world, than the most popular girl at Chatham Day!

When they had finished, Peg was reluctant to part from Pat. It was so pleasant talking to someone who cared for horses as much as she did. She lingered a little as Pat put the brushes in the empty bucket. "It was fun helping," she said. "Perhaps I'll see you tomorrow?"

Pat grinned at her. "I'm here every afternoon." Then, as if he regretted his friendliness, he snatched up the bucket and hurried out the door.

It had grown late while Peg helped Pat, and now she had time for only a quick canter on Merrylegs. Afterward she hurriedly stabled the pony, with frequent glances at her watch. Mother and Carol already disapproved of her visits to the stables—it would never do to be tardy to dinner!

Peg was perspiring from her furious pedaling when she slipped in the back door. "Is that you, Peg?" called a voice. "Come here." Mother! Peg reluctantly followed the voice to the front hall. Her mother was taking off her blue veiled hat in front of the hall mirror, fluffing her blond curls with a well-manicured hand. Turning, she exclaimed sharply, "Peg, what are you doing in those dreadful jodhpurs? I thought you were going to the country club with Carol—weren't Doreen and Marjorie going to be there too?"

Remembering her new resolution, Peg lifted her head defiantly. "I'm through with Doreen and Marjorie!" she cried, stomping her booted foot for emphasis. "They're nothing but a pair of nasty old fakes!"

"Peg! Really!" her mother exclaimed in horror.

"They can go on trying to be glamour girls if that's how they get their kicks, but from now on I'm going to the stables every day! I'm going to help Pat take care of the horses! I'm going to learn everything about horses and never spend a second more in a skirt than I have to!" With that, Peg raced up the stairs, ignoring her mother's shocked exclamations.

"Horses! Not again! And who is *Pat?*"

Once safely in her room, Peg began to calm down. She hoped Dad could smooth things over. He seemed to understand that she was different from other girls. She took off her riding boots, grabbed a book off the nightstand, and curled up on her bed. Whenever life seemed too hard to bear, Peg always chose the same book, and it didn't matter how many times she'd read it, it always gave her the same wonderful shivery feeling. With a happy sigh, she opened the battered green cover of *Journey to a Horse.*

Dinner that night was a strained affair. Her mother and Carol, both tight-lipped, exchanged glances over Peg's head as she stolidly ate her pot roast and mashed potatoes. As Della cleared the plates, her father coughed once or twice and then said with the genial air which made him a top sales manager at Shandygaff Industries, "What's this about you missing the Junior Miss thingamajig at the country club, Peg? That's not very nice disappointing those gals, is it?"

"They're just a bunch of old snobs!" said Peg with feeling.

"Well, I like that," Carol exclaimed witheringly, laying down her fork. "Those are some of my very best friends you're talking about, not to mention me!"

"Peg, I don't know where you get this attitude!" their mother burst out. "Those girls are your classmates and friends; they're the kind of people we want to associate with. But you seem unwilling to cooperate! All your time is spent at the stables!"

"Aw, Peg's not doing any harm," Johnny put in his two cents. "She's got as much right as the next fellow to wear her silly jodhpurs."

"I think you should forbid her to go to the stables," Carol told their mother.

"Now, Carol," Peg's father broke in. "All things in moderation, as my old prof used to tell us. Say, I've got an idea!" Mr. Gardner said as Della handed him a fresh martini. "Peg can go to the stables, but only if"—he held up his hand as Peg let loose a squeal of pleasure—"she also does her part on the Fall Frolic at the country club. That's the Junior Miss project, isn't it, Carol? What do you say, Peg?"

Peg's face fell at the mention of the Fall Frolic, but she knew she didn't have a choice. After all, Daddy paid the monthly stable bill. "All right, Daddy," she said slowly.

"That's Daddy's girl!" he said with a loving smile of approval as Della placed dishes of lemon meringue pie in front of them.

The next few weeks Peg spent every afternoon except Thursdays at the stable. Slowly, Garbo's strained tendon recovered, and Pat began giving her a little light exercise, taking her for short rides around the stable grounds. Often

Peg, on Merrylegs, accompanied them. The two horses had become fast friends, and happy-go-lucky Merrylegs seemed to steady the nervous mare, who was prone to starting at even a falling leaf. Pat and Peg, too, had become closer than Peg had ever imagined a boy and girl could be. Pat listened sympathetically to Peg's accounts of her troubles with her mother, the country club, the Junior Miss League. In turn, Pat told Peg his dream of going to school to become a veterinarian after graduating from Consolidated High that year, though he continued to speak little of his home or family.

One afternoon Peg arrived at the stables as Pat was leading Garbo out to the arena. "What's going on, Pat?" Peg queried excitedly.

"The vet came yesterday, and said Garbo's tendon was well enough for more exercise," Pat responded. "I'm going to start working her on the jumps—want to watch?"

"Of course!" Peg affirmed. She swung astride the fence and perched there, watching Pat put Garbo through her paces. Pat had Garbo on a lunging rein, and he circled her at a walk before cracking the whip sharply to cue Garbo into a brisk trot. Then again he snapped the whip, and Garbo broke into an even, flowing canter. Peg's throat ached with the beauty and grace of the dappled gray horse.

"Now let's try her on the jumps," Pat said after a few more circles. Still keeping the horse on the lunging rein, he guided her over the first jump. Effortlessly, Garbo gathered her legs beneath her and cleared the hurdle with room to spare.

Peg couldn't help clapping her hands. "Mrs. Huntley's going to be so pleased!"

Pat saddled Garbo up, circled the arena, and headed for

the jump. But just before the fence, Garbo came to a dead stop, nearly throwing Pat from the saddle. Pat took her back around, and again Garbo refused.

"I don't understand," said Pat, perplexed.

"Maybe something spooked her," suggested Peg.

"She didn't act spooked," Pat worried. "She just didn't want to take those jumps. I wish we knew what it was that circus clown did to her."

Peg thought about those clowns—the big red shoes they wore, their coarsely drawn mouths, the tiny cars they drove—and shuddered. Suddenly she had an idea. "Let me try something," she begged.

"What are you going to do?" Pat asked. "You're not an experienced jumper. I don't want you to get hurt."

"Nothing ventured, nothing gained," Peg shot back, quoting her father, and she ran to the stables. Quickly throwing a halter on Merrylegs, she led the dozing pony into the ring and tied her to the fence rail. Garbo grew visibly calmer. Peg mounted Garbo, and spurred her toward the jump. The horse took the hurdle with the same ease she had riderless and, without hesitating, turned toward the double jump. The horse and girl rode around the ring, Garbo taking all the jumps flawlessly, and then Peg slowed the horse and posted over to Pat. Pat's eyes were shining.

"I wish I'd had a stopwatch!" he declared. "I'll bet you'd have beat the blue-ribbon winner at last year's meet. You're a natural jumper, Peg!"

Laughing and blushing at Pat's extravagant compliment, Peg slid off the horse. She stumbled slightly, and Pat steadied her, his strong hands grasping her arms. For a moment blue eyes met gray eyes, and then Peg lowcred her gaze. She began to chatter nervously. "I wish dancing were as easy as jumping. I'm an awful dancer. I feel so awkward and I'm always taller than my partners."

"I know just how you feel," Pat said with complete understanding.

"Really?" Peg said, puzzled.

"Yes, my—my sister's quite tall," Pat quickly explained. Peg wished that she could meet Pat's tall, horse-loving sister—it seemed as if they had so much in common! Pat's next words broke in on Peg's thoughts.

"Look, Peg, I'm no great shakes, but I can give you a whirl if you want to practice some of those dances. What do you say?"

"Gee, Pat," said Peg, blushing a little, "that would be swell!"

Pat led her to a darkened corner of the feed room, empty now before the monthly oat delivery. He switched on the small transistor radio, and twisted the dial until he found a slow fox-trot, then he took Peg in his arms. Pat held her firmly, and Peg responded immediately to the lightest pressure from his hand on the small of her back, the way Garbo responded to the pressure of Peg's knees. To Peg, the smell of oats was better than the scent of flowers, and her feet felt lighter in her riding boots than they ever had in her pink evening shoes. She wished the dance would never end, that she and Pat could dance on and on, cheek to cheek. But at last the music swelled to a conclusion, and for a moment they stood in the circle of each other's arms. "Those kids in your dance class don't know anything," said Pat, a little gruffly. "You have a natural sense of rhythm."

"I guess I've just found the right partner," Peg said, boldly laying her head on his chest. But Pat flinched away.

"C-c-careful," he stuttered. "I have a sore spot there." The moment was over, and when they said goodbye and Peg wheeled her bike up the drive, it was almost as if the dance had never happened. Yet in her bed that night, *Journey to a Horse* discarded by her side, Peg kept reliving those minutes when she had been in Pat's arms. Suddenly, a daring plan came into her head—she would ask Pat to the Fall Frolic!

In the light of day, Peg was not so sure about her plan. She had never asked a boy to anything in her life. And Pat was sometimes so strangely distant—did he really like her as much as she liked him? Peg was still pondering her dilemma that afternoon as she worked attaching paper edelweiss to long lengths of green wire. Her thoughts were so intent on Pat that Nancy, the head of the decorations committee, had to call her name twice before she looked up. "Hey, Peg, come back from dreamland," Nancy chided her. "I asked you if you'd gotten your frock for the Frolic yet?"

"Oh, sorry!" Peg exclaimed.

"Peg was dreaming about her date," Doreen said with a spiteful giggle.

"Yes, Peg, is he a bay, or a chestnut?" Marjorie chimed in, and the two of them collapsed in helpless laughter.

Wooden-faced, Peg continued twisting wires together as Nancy tactfully changed the subject. Inside she vowed to herself, "I'm tired of being the odd girl out. I *will* invite Pat to the Fall Frolic, and I'll show them all!"

The next day at the stables, Peg marched up to Pat before she could lose her nerve, and said nervously, "Pat, would you be my date for the Fall Frolic?"

The saddle soap fell from Pat's grasp and he bent to pick it up. When he looked at Peg again, his face was unreadable. "I'd like to, Peg," Pat began, "but I'm afraid it's impossible."

"Never mind!" Peg said, humiliated. "I—I've got to go curry Merrylegs!" Awkwardly, she backed out of the stall, her cheeks crimson. She suddenly realized that a boy as handsome as Pat was sure to have a girl in Havertown.

"Wait a second, Peg." Pat caught up with her as she reached the tack room, and grasped her arm. "You don't understand—I really do want to take you to the Frolic. But I wouldn't be doing you any favor if I did."

Peg furrowed her brow. What could Pat mean? Then suddenly she knew! He'd heard her talking often enough about her mother and Carol to know what *they'd* think of a Polish stableboy from Havertown escorting her to the country club.

Looking deeply into his gray eyes, she said, "Oh, Pat, I know we come from different backgrounds, but let's not let other people's foolish prejudices get in our way. Besides, you'd help me show Doreen and Marjorie I'm not a social washout! They'd never expect me to snag an escort as good-looking as you!"

"Well, I've always dreamed of escorting a girl to a country club dance," Pat said slowly, a strange gleam in his eye. "And I'm just as eager to put those two in their places as you are. I'll rent a tux and—and shave, and all that stuff, and get you a corsage . . . Say, what color is your dress?"

"Midnight blue," Peg said.

"Then I'll get you gardenias. Greta Garbo loves gardenias. It will be like having Garbo there with us."

"Oh yes! That sounds wonderful," Peg sighed.

Pat put his arms around her. Peg felt herself tingle all over, as if she'd been plugged into an electric socket. Then suddenly, Pat's smile disappeared and Peg looked up into gray eyes that were clouded with concern. "Listen, Peg," Pat said slowly, "there's a couple of things I've got to get off my chest. Maybe you'll hate me, but—"

Just then they heard a voice calling, "Peg! Peg, dear, where are you?"

"That's Mother," Peg breathed. Pat swiftly released her and, grabbing a shovel, disappeared into the barn. Peg sighed as she watched her mother approach, picking her way gingerly through the piles of horse dung. "Drat this luck!" she thought. She hoped Pat would learn to forget about the social barriers between them. And what had he been about to tell her?

"There you are!" her mother exclaimed. "Hurry up, Peg, and get in the car. Uncle Roger's back from the Orient and he's coming down for a visit. We're going to pick him up at the station."

This wonderful news distracted Peg from her conversation with Pat. Everyone in the family loved glamorous Uncle Roger, the foreign exchange man for an important New York bank. He always came laden with exotic presents for the whole family. And Peg had a special relationship with him, for he shared her love of horses, and had helped her choose Merrylegs. Eagerly she climbed into the tan and white Buick and they set off for the station.

Uncle Roger was waiting for them, looking tanned and fit. It wasn't until they returned to the house on Meadowbrook Lane and Uncle Roger and Mother were having highballs that the Fall Frolic came up. "Tomorrow, Peg, you and I will have a grand ride and then I'll take you to dinner at the club, okay, pet?"

"Oh no, not tomorrow!" exclaimed Peg, suddenly remembering. "Tomorrow night's the Fall Frolic!"

"That's the Junior Miss dance at the country club," Peg's mother explained.

"Going to dances already! Who's your escort?" Uncle Roger inquired with interest.

"Her cousin Hank's going to take her," Mrs. Gardner murmured, making an expressive, let's-not-talk-about-it gesture.

"Oh, no, Mother!" Peg said. "I forgot to tell you when I heard about Uncle Roger coming, but I'm going with Pat."

"Pat!" said her mother with distaste. "The stableboy?"

Seeing Peg's distress and his sister's mounting irritation, Roger hastened to intervene. "Now, now, Helen!" he chided his sister, shaking a finger in mock reproof. "Don't be such a snob. The world is full of perfectly divine stableboys. Believe me, I know." Turning to Peg, he said, "Since tomorrow night is out, how about lunch at the club on Sunday? And why don't you invite your friend Pat as well? I'd like to meet him."

"Oh, thank you, Uncle Roger!" Peg cried gratefully. Then Johnny and Carol arrived, clamoring for presents, followed by Mr. Gardner, who promptly mixed up a fresh round of highballs, and the Fall Frolic was forgotten. In bed that night, Peg reflected that she had Uncle Roger to thank for smoothing things over with Mother. Peg was hurt by her mother's attitude, but she was too busy puzzling over Pat's secret to dwell on it. She had to talk to Pat and find out what he wanted to tell her, before the Frolic.

The next day, events conspired against Peg. Her mother had made an appointment for her at the hairdresser's in the morning, and she had to help with decorations in the afternoon. She hurried home, hoping to bike over to the stables for just a few minutes with Pat, but her mother was having a cocktail party for Uncle Roger and she was needed to help pass the canapés. Peg tried to telephone Pat, but infuriatingly, the only Kowalski in the Havertown directory didn't answer. Peg resigned herself to waiting for the evening.

Shortly before 7:30, Peg emerged from the bathroom. She had managed to tame her unruly red curls, and her new formal of midnight blue chiffon edged with navy velvet accentuated her creamy skin and candid blue eyes.

"You look lovely, dear," her mother approved as Carol flounced past her into the bathroom.

"You're not the only one going to the dance!" Carol snapped.

Peg wandered into her bedroom, too nervous of crushing her dress to sit down, her heart and head a dizzy whirl of hope and fear. Would Pat's rented tux fit? Would her parents embarrass her by asking him patronizing questions about Consolidated High? Would Carol snub him? And when they got to the dance and he saw the smooth girls like Marjorie and Doreen, would he regret bringing Peg? Absentmindedly, she dabbed a little eau de toilette on her wrists. *Ding dong!* Peg's heart jumped as she heard the door open, her father's hearty welcome, and her mother's more subdued voice.

Carol knocked on the door. "Your date's here, Peg," she said. "He's not bad-looking. It's too awful he has to work at those smelly stables." She turned on her heel with a swish of her pink tulle formal, while Peg bit back the furious retort that had leapt to her lips. The anger made her cheeks flush and her eyes sparkle, and she had never looked as lovely as she did entering the living room to greet Pat.

The men rose swiftly to their feet, Pat looking tall and handsome in a perfectly fitting tux and Peg's father nearly spilling his rob roy in an overflow of filial pride. "There's a fine-looking filly, hey, Pat?" her father exclaimed with a jocular nudge.

"A thoroughbred," said Pat seriously.

"Pat," purred Peg's mother, patting the sofa cushion beside her, "come sit here by me while Rob warms up the sedan."

"I drove here in the family station wagon," said Pat. "And I hope you'll trust me to drive Peg to the Frolic and back. I've had my license for over a year, and no violations."

Peg noted with pride the dignified way Pat made his request. She did so hope Daddy would consent. "What do you think, Helen?" he said genially as he freshened his drink.

"Pat looks like a fine young man," Peg's mother said, gazing at him with frank admiration. "I expect to see this young lady back by midnight! No excuses now!"

Peg's father shook hands vigorously with Pat, wincing a little at the strength of his grip. "All that mucking," thought Peg knowingly.

"You were wonderful," Peg declared with delight as the door closed behind them. "I could tell my parents liked you. Especially Mother." Pat opened the passenger door of the paneled station wagon for Peg, and then went around to the driver's side. With practiced ease he put the car into gear. As they pulled out of the driveway, Peg said, "I've been wanting to ask you something, Pat. What was it you were trying to tell me yesterday?"

"Later Peg, later," said Pat, taking her hand in his right hand and steering with his left. "I don't want anything to spoil this night." Pat gave Peg's hand a squeeze, and added in an undertone Peg could scarcely hear, "One night of happiness is worth years of pain and suffering."

Peg decided to ignore Pat's mysterious addendum, and boldly, she squeezed Pat's hand in return. Before she knew it, they were at the country club. Inside, they checked Pat's overcoat and Peg's velvet wrap with a charming brunette, one of the Junior Miss volunteers. Peg was glad now that she had done her volunteer stint helping with decorations and could enjoy an evening of uninterrupted pleasure. They entered the ballroom, transformed into a tiny alpine village by the hard work of the decorating committee. With a smile, Pat held out his arms and swept Peg onto the floor to a lilting waltz. As they whirled between papier-mâché Alps, under glittering festoons of cuckoo clocks, Peg was oblivious to the admiring and envious glances that followed them, her eyes only on Pat. When the dance ended, they applauded enthusiastically, and then strolled to a table shaped like a giant wheel of Swiss cheese, with a vivacious blonde standing in one of the holes, serving punch.

At a tap on her shoulder, Peg turned to see Marjorie, in a strapless formal of scotch-plaid taffeta, beaming with false cordiality. "Peg! You look divine!" she gushed. In a stage whisper clearly meant to be heard, she added, "Introduce me to your handsome escort!" Peg made the introduction reluctantly. "Marjorie, I'd like you to meet my friend Pat Kowalski. Marjorie Briarcliffe, a classmate of mine." "How do you do," said Pat, taking the hand Marjorie extended. Doreen hurried up too, in lime green. Peg was edged away from Pat as he was caught up in a gale of vivacious chatter and laughter. She couldn't hear what they were saying as a crowd of boys gathered around her eagerly.

"Want to give this one a whirl?" asked Biff, Marjorie's date and the star halfback of Chatham Day. Peg couldn't help but feel a thrill of triumph when she caught Carol staring open-mouthed and Fred looking Peg up and down as if seeing her for the first time. Biff was waiting for an answer, but Peg realized that, flattered as she was, she didn't want to dance with anyone but Pat!

As if in answer to her thoughts, Pat appeared at Peg's side. "Sorry, big fella," he said pleasantly, "this is our dance." As he swept Peg away once more, she heard Biff complaining, "What's he got that I don't?"

Jealously, Pat kept Peg to himself all evening. When Carol's date, Fred, was quick enough to claim her at the beginning of a dance, Pat selected one of the perennial wallflowers, leaving Carol fuming. And when Fred tried to get too familiar, Pat appeared instantly, cutting in.

Finally they stopped to catch their breath on one of the rustic benches. "If only Garbo were here!" Peg exclaimed.

"Speaking of Garbo, Mrs. Huntley and I have a little surprise for you," Pat said with a special smile. "We've decided that you'll be the one to show Garbo—if that's okay with you, that is."

"Oh yes," Peg breathed. She turned and looked at the dance floor, wondering if anyone there could be happier than she was at this moment. There were Chet and Doreen, laughing by the punch bowl. And Fred, struggling to pull Carol closer as they danced. She spotted Mr. Carter, the club's golf pro, wearing the same festive lederhosen as the other chaperones. "Why, look," she said, pointing. "There's Marlene with Pete Davis. Doesn't he go to Consolidated too?"

Abruptly Pat stood up, pulling Peg to her feet. "Let's go out on the terrace and get some fresh air," he said. Peg followed him obediently. She guessed it *had* been rude of her to have pointed so blatantly. Outside they stopped by the box hedge and gazed at the twinkling stars.

"Oh dear!" she said. "Soon we'll have to go. It's past eleven, isn't it?"

"Yes, you're right, we'll have to go pretty soon," Pat replied with an echoing sigh.

"Well," said Peg, trying to cheer herself, "there will be other nights." When Pat didn't say anything, she asked hesitantly, "Won't there?"

"Yes, I guess so," said Pat, forcing a smile, "but never another night like this." After a moment he shook off the mysterious sorrow that always seemed to shadow him. "Why, you're shivering." Taking off his dinner jacket, he wrapped it around Peg and pulled her close. Peg gazed into his somber gray eyes, and then their lips touched. Their kiss was everything Peg had always known it would be, and as they leaned into the box hedge, the leaves quivered with sympathetic passion. Suddenly, they heard voices nearby breaking into their romantic idyll.

"I knew 'he' looked familiar!" a boy's voice exclaimed. "That's no 'he'! That's Patty Kowalski—she's in my biology class at Consolidated!"

In a daze, Peg backed away from Pat, whose face had drained of all color. A murmur broke from the crowd of boys and girls gathering around Pete Wilson, as Pat and Peg emerged from the shelter of the box hedge. Biff and Marjorie, Chet and Doreen, Carol and Fred were all there. The boys stepped forward. "I think you'd better beat it, chum," said Biff threateningly. "We don't go for these Havertown kind of pranks in Chatham!"

"A rumble!" thought Peg, horrified. Desperately, she tried to recall an article about ju-jitsu she had read in the *National Geographic*. But before anyone had a chance to start anything, Miss Maney, the jovial phys ed teacher and one of the Frolic's chaperones, came hurrying over.

"What's going on here, kids?" Miss Maney boomed. A chorus of voices answered her, "That boy's a girl!" "Peg brought another girl to the Frolic!" Miss Maney quickly realized she'd better put the lid on this potential country club scandal, and she grasped Pat's arm. "I'll escort you to your car," she said, not unkindly. "And we'll discuss this prank of yours." Pat turned and looked pleadingly at Peg as Miss Maney led her away. Peg stared back, still dumbstruck. Her thoughts were in a whirl, but the one thing that stood out clearly was that Pat, the person she had most trusted and loved, had deceived her. The other boys and girls began to drift away, stealing curious glances at Peg, who stood like a stone on the terrace.

"Come along, Peg, Fred and I will take you home," Carol said pityingly.

"Come on, Peg, there's always room for a threesome in my car," added Fred with a leer, as Carol flashed him an angry look.

"I'll take a taxi," Peg choked out. Blindly she fled across the terrace, Carol's reply floating after her. "That's what comes of dating out of your class!"

Once at home, safe in her room, Peg wept, for the beautiful friendship which now must cease to be, and for Pat's betrayal, which turned her most precious memories into ashes. She wept as she removed the midnight blue formal and cold-creamed her face, clad in her nightgown and quilted bathrobe. When at last it seemed she must have drained herself dry of tears, she went down to the kitchen to get a snack. What with her nervous anticipation earlier—it seemed eons ago to Peg—she hadn't had much supper. She fixed herself a liverwurst sandwich and poured a big glass of milk. Her tears welled up again as she remembered sharing a potted meat sandwich with Pat at the stable. Why, oh why hadn't Pat told her the truth? Why hadn't she trusted Peg?

At the sound of a soft footfall, Peg turned. Her Uncle Roger was standing in the doorway, his handsome face creased with concern. "Now, now, what's all this about?" he said, sitting down next to her. "Didn't your date go well?"

"I had a wonderful time," Peg sobbed, "but then I found out that Pat's a girl!"

"My, that must have been a shock!" said Uncle Roger. "How did you find out?"

Peg told him the story of the evening, and Uncle Roger listened intently.

"Why didn't she tell me?" Peg asked Uncle Roger. "Why did she have to lie to me that way?"

Uncle Roger patted her consolingly. "Don't be too hard on her, Peg. She probably didn't mean to deceive you. She had to disguise herself as a boy to get the job at the stables, and that meant fooling everyone, you included." Uncle Roger gave Peg a quick history of cross-dressing from the Ancients through Shakespeare and the modern age, then concluded, "I think, Peg, that Pat really does care for you. She took you to the dance, despite the risk, because she thought it would make *you* happy."

As Peg thought over Uncle Roger's words, her indignation subsided. What Pat must have been going through all those times that she'd been chattering away about her own petty problems! The liverwurst sandwich forgotten on her plate, Peg cried anew, this time tears of remorse.

"I've been so selfish!" she sobbed. "What can I do to make it up to Pat?"

Uncle Roger chuckled, a low warm sound. "Why don't you ask her? Remember, you're both having lunch with me at the country club tomorrow. And I'll be very hurt if I'm stood up!" He pulled a handkerchief from his dressing-gown pocket and handed it to Peg. "Wipe your eyes now, and get some sleep."

But Peg lay in her snug bed a long time before sleep came, unable to forget the pleading look in Pat's gray eyes as Miss Maney led her away.

Peg's thoughts were so busy with Pat that she didn't realize that she might have other problems until she walked into the breakfast nook the next morning, where Carol and Johnny were having waffles, while their mother sipped a cup of coffee. Johnny exclaimed immediately, "Peggy's got a *girl*friend, Peggy's got a *girl*friend!"

"Stop that at once, Johnny!" Mrs. Gardner commanded. "If you're finished with your waffles, you may go outside and play baseball, or some other healthy sport."

Groaning, Johnny complied, letting the back door clatter noisily behind him.

"I must say I'm disappointed in you, Peg," said Mrs. Gardner, addressing Peg rather severely. "Della! Waffles for Peg!" she called toward the kitchen, then continued, "That was quite an extraordinary prank your friend pulled."

Peg morosely drenched the waffles Della brought with butter and syrup. "I suppose Carol told you all about it," she said.

Her mother leaned forward. "Did you know Pat was a girl, Peg?"

Carol snorted, "Of course she knew!"

"No, I didn't know!" cried Peg. "But now that I do, I don't care! Pat's still the swellest person I've ever known! And he's—she's much more of a gentleman than Fred."

"That's a lie!" Carol said, the fury in her voice belying her words. Mrs. Gardner looked from one face to the other. "Run into the yard and pick some flowers for luncheon, Carol. You know Roger loves those yummy autumnal arrangements of yours. I want to talk to Peg alone."

Unwillingly Carol left the breakfast nook, closing the back door carefully behind her.

"Now, what's this about Fred?" said Peg's mother.

As Peg described Fred's lecherous manner, her mother grew flushed, her eyes gleaming, as she listened avidly. "Shocking, shocking—why, the very idea," she murmured. "I'll have Carol ask him over to the house, and I'll have a talk with him."

"I don't want to see him!" Peg said in disgust.

"You won't have to, dear." Mrs. Gardner patted Peg reassuringly. "I'll choose a time when no one else is around."

Uncle Roger came into the breakfast nook still clad in his maroon and gold striped silk dressing gown, yawning widely. "Oh, this country air!" he exclaimed. "Makes me sleep like a horse!"

"I think the figure of speech is 'eat like a horse.' " His sister laughed. "Shall I have Della warm up some waffles?"

"No, thanks, I'll just have a cup of coffee. Must watch my waistline. Speaking of horses"—Uncle Roger turned to Peg—"I'll pick you and Pat up at the stables at noon."

"I don't know if this—this Patricia is the kind of friend we want Peg associating with," Mrs. Gardner began.

"Oh, now, Helen, the girls haven't done any harm," Uncle Roger protested.

"And I have to confess that I'd be relieved if my little girl put off dating boys for just a bit longer," added Mr. Gardner as he entered the kitchen, one of Della's famous Bloody Marys in hand.

"I suppose Father knows best," Mrs. Gardner relented with a smile. "I must speak to Carol now, arrange for a tête-à-tête with Fred."

As she left, Uncle Roger shook his finger at Peg. "And don't you have a tête-à-tête as well? Scat!"

Peg biked to the stables a trifle more slowly than usual. She longed to see Pat, yet she also dreaded the encounter. As she biked under the wooden sign, she saw Mrs. Huntley striding toward the little office.

"Mrs. Huntley!" she called. "Is Pat here?"

"Yes, Peg, she's here. She's in Garbo's stall, saying goodbye."

"Goodbye!" gasped Peg. "You're not—you're not going to fire her just because she's a girl!"

"Girl or not, she's the best stableboy I've ever had," Mrs. Huntley replied. "Pat's quitting. I'm not sure why." Continuing into the office, she said over her shoulder, "Maybe you can figure it out."

Peg sped into the stables and, like a homing pigeon, flew to Garbo's stall. Pat was there, her face buried in Garbo's neck. "Pat, you can't quit!" Peg exclaimed. Pat jerked around and Peg's eyes widened. Now she understood that sore spot on Pat's chest. With an effort, she pulled her eyes back to Pat's face and continued. "You're the best stable—stable *something* this place has ever had!"

"What are you doing here?" he—no, *she*—demanded.

"I came to find you," said Peg. "My uncle's taking us to lunch at the country club, remember?"

"I thought you'd never want to talk to me again," Pat muttered, turning away.

"Oh, Pat, don't be silly." Peg's voice shook. "I feel terrible about last night. I was such a dope. I'd feel the same way about you if you were a girl or a boy or . . . or a horse!"

"I was going to quit because I knew coming to the stables would only remind me of you—" She turned toward Peg, her gray eyes full of unshed tears. Peg stared back, unsure of what to do next. Suddenly, with an anxious whicker, Garbo nudged Pat toward the lanky redhead. Then Pat's arms were around Peg, and when their lips met, Peg knew that everything was all right again.

"Pat." Mrs. Huntley's jovial voice broke into their tender interlude. "There are stalls to be mucked out—that is," she added, peering into the stall with a smile, "if you *are* still working here!"

"Yes, ma'am!" exclaimed Pat, and they all laughed together. Peg helped Pat clean stalls and the morning flew by. When Uncle Roger telegraphed his approval of Pat with winks and nods as he drove them to the country club, Peg thought she couldn't contain any more happiness. Luncheon was gay, with Uncle Roger telling funny stories of his adventures in Hong Kong over the Caesar salads and roast beef. As the meat plates were cleared away, Uncle Roger questioned Pat about her ambition to be a veterinarian. "My roommate, Bruce, knows some people at Cornell," said Uncle Roger. "Maybe you and Peg should come to the city for a weekend sometime, and we could arrange a chat. How would you like that?"

Peg met Pat's glance, each filled with delight. "That

sounds lovely, Uncle Roger!" cried Peg. "When you're a vet, Pat, you can tend to the horses in my stable!"

"Wonderful idea," approved Uncle Roger. "Ah," he said as three plates of floating island were set flaming before them, "now this is something like it!"

Pastures of Passion

Squ-e-e-e-al! Oreola woke up with a start as the automobile came to a sudden stop. She peered through the dust-covered window and saw that Pa and Uncle Jo-Jo had already gotten out and were looking under the hood of the old Model-T. "Might be a piece of tumbleweed got kinda twisted 'round the rear axle agin', like in Sweetwater," she heard Uncle Jo-Jo suggest. Pa said nothing. He just sighed and got down on his hands and knees to crawl under the jalopy.

"Orie, I'm going to see if your pa needs help. You keep an eye on the young'uns," said Oreola's mother, struggling out from under a pile of bedding in the front seat. The whole car was stuffed so full of their belongings, the clothing, farm-tools, and the bits of furniture they'd been able to take from the farm in Oklahoma after the bank foreclosed, that there was hardly any room for Ma, Pa, Uncle Jo-Jo, the five Budd children, and Grandma Jennie.

Grandma Jennie sat at the other end of the backseat from Oreola, knitting and sucking her toothless gums. In between her and Oreola were the four little Budds—Jeff, the twins Bob and Bunnie, and little Loula Mae Budd, who was only two. Now all of them were awake, whimpering and fidgeting so that Oreola could hardly stand it.

"Grandma Jennie, I'm goin' to climb up top and git me some fresh air," said Oreola. "Likely we'll be here for some time."

Grandma Jennie nodded and cackled to herself in that way she had. Oreola cranked down the window, squeezed out from under the rolled-up rug that lay across the little Budds, and nimbly climbed through the opening. Getting a foothold on the rearview mirror, she grasped onto the tie ropes and pulled herself to the top of the car, where the mattresses were piled. Way up there, Oreola could feel a faint cool breeze. She lay back on the topmost mattress and tried to imagine, for the thousandth time, what California would be like.

For the last year, the family had talked of little else besides California—how green it was, how the fruit practically fell off the trees right into your mouth, how a man could find enough work there to feed his family—unlike Oklahoma, where crops and jobs and whole families had just disappeared in a cloud of red dust these past few years. Of all the Budd children, only Oreola could even remember a time when there'd been green on their farm and more to eat than grits. Oreola thought about the raisin that each of the Budd children had found in their Christmas stockings this past year. The little ones had gobbled theirs up straightaway and then cried when it was all gone. Oreola had meant to save her raisin for something special but, in the end, had divided it up so that her little brothers and sisters could each get one more sweet taste.

Since they'd set out, two weeks earlier, the whole family

had made a game out of saying what they all hoped for when they got to California. Pa hoped to make enough money to buy a new farm and Ma hoped for a new dress, her first since before Oreola was born. Uncle Jo-Jo said how he'd heard they had some mighty pretty gals out in California and maybe he could meet himself one who wouldn't hold it against a feller if he'd spent a little stretch in the state pen. Grandma Jennie hoped she could get herself some new teeth and Jeff, Bob, and Bunnie never stopped talking about raisins. Only Loula Mae and Oreola never joined in, Loula Mae because she was too young to talk much yet, and Oreola because she was too shy to say that the only thing she hoped for was a best friend.

When Oreola was nine, she had read a story in her school reader about two girls who were best friends. They had gone for walks together and combed each other's hair and told each other everything. Oreola had known that she would never be best friends with any of the girls in her class—Sissy Jenkins was too stuck-up, Betsy Pearson was mean as a rattlesnake, and Evie Sue Tyler just wasn't right in the head—but she had hoped that maybe some new girl would come to the school to be her best friend. Then the money to pay Miss Littleton had run out and the school had closed.

That had been three years ago, but Oreola had never stopped thinking about it. She'd even fashioned herself a doll out of a corn cob, some straw, and a couple of lima beans and named it Annie, like one of the girls in the book. Oreola looked wistfully down at Annie, whom she always kept close at hand, and smoothed down the few strands of straw that served as her hair. Yes, California was sure to be better.

They were somewhere in Texas now and Pa had heard that cotton pickers were making 14 cents a bale. He hoped to make enough money to get them a piece farther along the road to California, but when Oreola sat up and looked around from her perch atop the car, all she saw were fields of brown grass, in all directions.

Then Oreola's eyes were caught by a movement. There was a little black foal in one of the fields, switching his tail back and forth as he nosed at the long grass. As she watched, the foal kicked up his hind legs and ran in a little circle.

Oreola slid off the mattress and landed lightly in the dirt by the side of the road. Her bare feet made no sound as she ran through the grass toward the little foal. But the horse sensed her coming and, with a funny snort, kicked up his heels and trotted away. "Wait, little horsey, wait!" cried Oreola, running after him. But the little horse was too fast. With a whinny, he threw up his heels and disappeared in the tall grass.

Then Oreola heard a distant put-put-put. Pa and Uncle Jo-Jo must have gotten the old Model-T started again! Turning around, she realized she'd traveled quite a piece from the road, chasing the horse. The auto was small in the distance, and as she hurried back across the fields, she saw the old car move slowly forward. "Wait, wait!" she screamed, running and stumbling through the field. But the car put-put-putted down the road, and soon disappeared over a small rise. Oreola sank down in the grass. She often rode on the mattresses up on top of the car—no one would realize that she wasn't there until they stopped for the night. How would they ever find her again? She began to cry bitterly.

"*Que pasa?*" said a voice quite near her. Oreola scrambled to her feet. A Mexican girl her own age, as short and plump as Oreola was tall and lanky, pushed her way through the tall grass. The girl had wavy black hair, covered with a red kerchief, and big brown eyes, which examined Oreola with friendly curiosity. "Who are you?" the girl asked in English.

Oreola wiped away her tears. "I'm Oreola Budd."

"And what is that you are holding?" the girl inquired.

Oreola looked down to see that she was still clutching Annie in her hand. The sight of the doll made Oreola acutely conscious of her twelve years. "It's jist a doll," she replied, trying to take on a careless tone.

"A doll? But it is nothing more than a corn cob with some straw," the strange girl said, puzzled.

"No, looka here. Don't you see she got lima bean eyes?" Oreola explained. "Her name is Annie."

The girl peered closely at Annie. "Ohhhh!" she said admiringly. "Now I see." She smiled broadly, adding, "And her name is nearly the same as mine! I am Ana Maria Leticia Ortiz."

Oreola stared, disbelieving. Could this be her Annie? And she hadn't even had to go to California to find her, she thought wonderingly. Thinking of California, Oreola remembered her plight and the tears flowed down her cheeks again.

"What is wrong, Oreola?" Ana Maria asked sympathetically.

"I was traveling through with my family, but they done gone off and left me."

"Pobrecita!" said the other girl, taking her hand. "You can stay with us."

There was a rustling sound, and the little black foal poked his head through the grass.

"El Cid! You bad one! I have been looking for you," scolded Ana Maria. The foal nuzzled her cheek, until she giggled.

"Is this horse yours?" exclaimed Oreola. Her words tumbled over each other as she told the Mexican girl how she had followed the foal and so been left behind.

"El Cid belongs to my family," said the girl, hugging the foal. "Come home with me, and I will show you the tricks I have taught him."

Willingly Oreola followed Ana Maria. Being left behind did not seem so bad, now that she had made the acquaintance of the mischievous black foal and the friendly Mexican girl with the wonderful name.

Soon they reached the farmyard of a small white frame house, which was bursting at the seams with black-eyed, black-haired children, Ana Maria's brothers and sisters and cousins. Her uncle and her father had adjoining farms, Ana Maria explained, and everyone helped out on both. "We have to work very hard to pay the bank loan," said Ana Maria.

Oreola nodded sadly. "You-all are sure lucky you still have a farm," she said.

Oreola stood back bashfully as Ana Maria helped the women prepare dinner, enjoying the way they cheerfully laughed and chattered in Spanish. Her mouth watered at the many new and enticing smells. When the Ortiz clan seated themselves at the table, Ana Maria pulled Oreola into a chair next to hers. Oreola could hardly wait to dig in, but it was all so strange, she began to feel awkward. She picked up an unfamiliar implement and whispered to Ana Maria, "How does this-here thingamabob work?"

"This? But this is just a fork! Have you not seen one before?" responded Ana Maria, incredulous.

"We warn't fancy at home," Oreola explained. "We never needed more'n a spoon."

Ana Maria patiently explained the use of the fork and knife to Oreola, who found them quite useful for digging into the heaping plate of food in front of her. All of the food was delicious, but best of all were Mama Ortiz's tamales.

"They are famous through all the county," said Ana Maria proudly. "There is no one who makes a better tamale than *mi madre.*"

After dinner, Ana Maria took Oreola out to watch El Cid play in the corral. As they perched on the fence and watched the spirited foal, Ana Maria told Oreola her dream was to someday compete with El Cid in the barrel racing competition in Austin. "It is the biggest rodeo in all the state of Texas, and when El Cid and I win there, I am sure to find a job as a horse trainer."

In turn, Oreola confided to Ana Maria that she would one day like to be a nurse. "I know I'm a little short on readin' and writin' and figurin' and such," Oreola admitted, "but sometimes when the young'uns got hurt, I fixed 'em up and Ma always said I did a right fine job of it."

Later that night, when it was time for bed, Ana Maria asked Oreola if she would comb out her hair and offered to comb Oreola's. Oreola shivered with delight. She could hardly believe that it was all happening just like in the story. She finally, truly had a best friend! The girls snuggled down together in Ana Maria's bed, and whispered and giggled long into the night, even after they heard Mama Ortiz call sternly, "Ana Maria! Oreola! *Silencio!*"

Oreola woke the next morning to Mama Ortiz's call, "Oreola, *mija,* see who has come!" She flew down the stairs, with Ana Maria right behind her. There was the old

Model-T parked in the farmyard, and her ma and pa standing by it talking to Mr. Ortiz, while the little Budds stared out the window at all the Ortiz children who stared back at them. Mama cried and scolded Oreola, at the same time giving her a hug so tight Oreola could hardly breathe. Pa rested his hand on her head, and said only, "You caused us a peck o' worryin', Orie." They had driven back through the night, asking at all the farms along the road if anyone had seen a girl with yellow hair and cornflower blue eyes.

Oreola was happy her parents had found her, but she was happier still when she heard Mr. Ortiz telling her father about the big cotton farm only three miles away. They would have work for a month, and she and Ana Maria would see each other every day! Joyfully the two girls embraced, pressing each other to their budding bosoms.

As they chugged away, Pa remarked to Ma, "I guess them Mexicans ain't so different from the rest of us."

Ma replied, "Yep, the Lord visits hard times on the white people and the brown people just the same."

Pa laughed grimly. "Or the bank does."

The month flew by all too soon. Every evening, Oreola would walk the three miles from the pickers' shacks to the Ortiz farm. It was a long walk after twelve backbreaking hours picking cotton, but when Oreola arrived at the Ortiz farm and heard El Cid's spirited whinny and saw Ana Maria running to greet her, her hair flying in the wind, she would feel renewed. As they diligently worked, training El Cid, the worries and hardships that filled the rest of Oreola's life lay outside the corral, forgotten.

Some evenings Ana Maria and Oreola would ride through the fields on Blaze, El Cid's mother. At first, Oreola had been afraid to climb up on the big mare—

she'd only ever ridden Sal, the stubborn old mule who had pulled her father's plow back in Oklahoma. But with Ana Maria's patient instruction, Oreola soon lost much of her nervousness. Still, when Blaze would leap over a ditch or shy from a tumbleweed, Oreola would clutch tightly around Ana Maria's waist, and not let go until the ride was over. Ana Maria never complained.

Finally the day came when all the cotton was picked, and Oreola had to say goodbye. She walked over early one morning to take her leave. She could stay only a little while, for she had to help Mama pack the Model-T and take care of the young Budds. Mama Ortiz wrapped a passel of her delicious tamales for the Budds' lunch, and Ana Maria and El Cid walked back with her through the fields.

"You will come back again next year, yes?" Ana Maria asked.

"I can see how we might jist do that," answered Oreola, barely getting the words out of her tightening throat. Many times over the last month Ana Maria had asked that same question, and Oreola had given the same answer. It was easier than facing the truth—Oreola knew that with the exciting new life that awaited them in California, her family would probably never want to leave.

"I wish we could stay in touch somehow," said Ana Maria.

"I'll write to you," promised Oreola. "And anytime we're settled for a little while, why, you can write to me."

"And when we're grown up, we'll live together," said Ana Maria for the hundredth time. "I'll train horses—"

"And I'll be a nurse!" finished Oreola. When the two girls had hugged each other for the last time, Oreola buried her face in El Cid's neck, so that Ana Maria would not see her tears. As the Budds' car pulled away, Oreola pressed her face against the dusty back window of the old Model-T, waving to Ana Maria until the girl and horse were nothing but two tiny specks covered in a cloud of dust. Oreola's greatest hope had been to find one best friend. Now she had to face the heartache of losing two.

Other heartaches followed. It soon became clear to Oreola and the rest of the Budd family that their golden dreams of California were nothing more than an illusion perpetuated by the big growers looking for cheap labor. And so they joined the growing tide of migrant workers, traveling up and down the San Joaquin Valley in a blur of oranges, beans, lettuce, tomatoes, and cauliflower.

But Oreola was writing faithfully every week to Ana Maria, and when they were settled anywhere for more than a few weeks, Ana Maria would write back. When Oreola's back was aching and her hands were blistered and cut up, it was good to lie on her straw pallet in the hen coop where the fruit pickers were lodged, and read about Ana Maria and the Ortiz family and El Cid.

Dear Oreola,

I miss you more than I can say, and it pains me to hear of your troubles. If I were there with you, I could at least rub a gentle salve onto your hands and back. Mama makes such a salve from aloe. I think you would find it very soothing.

El Cid is a yearling now and he is already smarter and faster than Mr. Pugh's pure-bred quarter horse. Mr. Pugh has again offered to buy him. I fear that he knows of our troubles paying the bank loan since his brother-in-law, Mr. Hammond, is the president of the bank, but

Papa promises me that he will not sell El Cid. When we win the barrel racing competition in Austin and I get a job as a horse trainer, we will no longer have to worry about the bank loan or Mr. Pugh. Then I will be able to pay for your nursing school and buy a little house where the two of us shall live together.

With all my love,
Ana Maria

Reading about Ana Maria's plans helped keep Oreola's spirits up as her family's situation grew increasingly worse.

Dear Ana Maria,

I shore do miss you. When I was pickin peaches yesterday, a drop of the juice fell into my mouth on accident and for some reason the sweet nectar set me to thinkin about the time we spent together. But then the nectar turned bitter in my mouth when they took the price of the peach out of my days wages.

It seems like we coudnt have got ourselves to California at a werse time. Theres so many folks comin from Oklahoma way lookin fer werk out here that the growers dont hardly have to pay a thing to git folks to do the werk. Now their payin us jist a penny a bushel for pickin peaches and with the whole family workin cept for Loula Mae and Bunnie we only made us three dollers last week. Pa ain't talkin about his farm so much or Ma about her new dress. Jeff and the twins gave up on tryin to save for a box of raisins when Loula Mae took sick and we had to spend their raisin money on the docter.

Love forever,
Oreola

Oreola reflected bitterly on the hardships her family had suffered at the hands of the bankers and now the growers. Miss Littleton, the schoolteacher back in Oklahoma, had taught that America was the land of opportunity. As smart as Miss Littleton was, Oreola couldn't help but think that maybe she was wrong about that. Oreola couldn't see that there was any opportunity for folks like her. It seemed that opportunity was only for those that already had land and money. These hard lessons might have driven all hope out of Oreola, if not for the letters from Ana Maria.

Dear Oreola,

El Cid has grown so swift that when I ride him, the wind feels like fingers running through my hair. I only wish that I were not riding alone. I remember how you used to hold on so tightly to me when we rode Blaze. How I wish you were here now.

Still there is no rain and most of my papa's crops have failed. Mama has started to sell her tamales at the market in town on Saturdays and I have taken a job in town, cleaning the house of Mr. Hammond. This leaves me less time to train El Cid, but without this money I fear that Papa would have to break his promise to me and sell El Cid.

Dear Ana Maria,

Is your hair still long and thick? You woudnt hardly recognize me now as short as mine is. All that hair dint do nothing but get in the way of pickin and such. It just warnt practical. I shore hope that yore hair is still as pretty as I remember it though.

Lately it seems like the growers have decided that they got too many crops. So what do you think they do about it? Give the food to them that needs it? No sirree, that aint what they do. These here growers burn up whole piles of food and I'll tell you it burns me *up.*

Dear Oreola,

I wish you had saved the golden tresses that you found so oppressive. I remember how lovely your hair looked when the setting sun would catch it. At least you can do nothing to change the blue of your eyes. I will take heart in that.

El Cid grows stronger and faster every day. We rode in our first barrel racing competition last week at the local rodeo in Wheeler and our time was the third fastest. Sadly, it grows ever more difficult to find time to spend with El Cid. In addition to cleaning Mr. Hammond's house, I have now begun to manage the finances of his household.

P.S. Sometimes when the prices are very low, the farmers are forced to limit production in order to artificially boost prices.

Dear Ana Maria,

I hope all that time yore spendin doing figures for Mr. Hammond aint too hard on yore eyes. I remember real clear how they looked like deep forest pools. It would be a real shame if anything happened to change that, so you be careful with them eyes.

I'm sorry to say I don't got much happy news to report. Uncle Jo-Jo got hisself landed in jail agin. Seems to me like he sniffs out trouble the way a dog sniffs out a bone, though maybe he jist didn't know that his new girlfriend was the sheriff's wife. Then Grandma Jennie up and died. It don't seem like she ever got that Oklahoma dust out of her lungs. We had to git the coffin at the company store, where they cost twice as much as the ones in town, but them town stores won't sell to the pickers on credit. P.S. I jist cain't see that what the growers need, when there's so few of them, should be more important than what the pickers need, when there's so awful many of us.

Dear Oreola,

I have found a way to spend more time with El Cid. Mr. Hammond's daughter, Katherine, wishes to learn how to ride, so part of my job now is teaching her. She has grown very fond of me and has been very kind, but I still think of you every day and miss you very much.

El Cid and I finished in first place at the county fair in Amarillo. I don't think there is a better barrel racer than El Cid in all of Texas.

Papa's crops did not do well again this year, but the whole family has been working very hard to keep up the loan payments. Jorge has started helping Papa in the fields and Juanita now keeps house for Mr. Pugh, but Mama's hands have been hurting her and she has not brought her tamales to market for several weeks.
P.S. Is it not so that an individual must live or die by the work of their own hand? Is that not what makes us free?

Dear Ana Maria,
We've moved to a new camp again. I do so wish that we could settle in one place for more than a month or two, if only so that it would be easier for your letters to find me. I've met a girl named Mary Sykes at this new camp and she and I have gotten friendly. It's nice to have someone to spend time with, but sometimes being with her only makes me miss you even more. Besides, once pea picking is over, we'll move on to a new crop, a new camp, and I'll find a new friend.
P.S. How can we be truly free if we are enslaved by the chains of capitalism?

Oreola, in the midst of writing a new letter to Ana Maria, stopped a moment and tried to count up the number of different camps they'd stayed at since their arrival in California. She stopped when she got to a dozen. And in each camp, there had been new people, a new crop, and usually, for Oreola, a new best friend. Would Ana Maria understand? None of these other girls could take her place, but Depression times were lonely times and a girl had to take comfort where she could. Oreola wondered what kind of comfort Katherine Hammond provided for Ana Maria.

As Oreola signed her usual "Love forever, Oreola" and put the letter in the envelope, she thought about how much she had changed since she and Ana Maria were last together. Five years of working in the fields had hardened her and these union folks she had met recently had changed her in other ways. They'd tutored her in reading and writing, but more importantly, they'd given her the words to better express the ideas that had been fermenting inside her since her arrival in California—words like "proletariat" and "bourgeoisie." How had Ana Maria changed in these last five years, Oreola wondered.

"Here's another letter for you, Orie." Loula Mae, now seven and old enough to join the rest of the family in the fields, interrupted Oreola's reverie. Oreola seized the envelope curiously. Another letter from Ana Maria! The letter Oreola had just finished was in response to one she'd received only three days ago. Oreola ripped open the envelope.

Dear Oreola,

Many things have happened since I last wrote. Mr. Hammond has bought a house in town for Katherine and she has ~~told me I must~~ asked me to come live there with her. She says that when I am living with her in town, she will tell her father to give me a job as a teller at his bank. I have told her that she is being too ~~insistent~~ generous, but she says that she is happy to do this for her best friend. I have explained to her ~~that~~

~~you will always be~~ ~~that I can never forget~~ that I still think of you as my best friend, but you have written about so many other friends, ~~you have probably moved on to~~ I wonder if you still feel this way about me. Next week is the state fair in Austin. After it is over, I will move into Katherine's house. ~~If only you could~~

We have fallen farther behind than ever in the loan payments and Mama's hands grow worse and worse. The doctor says that if we do not get her the medicine she needs, she may never be able to make tamales again. Mr. Pugh is now offering quite a handsome sum for El Cid and there is no room for El Cid at Katherine's house, so when the fair is over, I will sell him. ~~Though no one could pay enough to make up for the hearta~~

P.S. I am saddened by the communistic tone your letters have taken and curious about your greatly improved grammar and spelling. I hope your new friend is treating you ~~more loyally than~~ ~~as well as I~~ kindly.

Love forever,
Ana Maria

Tears blurred Oreola's vision as she read the letter, which was already hard enough to read, it was so stained and full of cross-outs. What on earth had prompted Ana Maria to accept this banker's daughter's perfidious proposition? And how could she think about selling El Cid? Oreola had always cherished the dream that one day she and Ana Maria and El Cid would make a home together.

Over the years the dream had faded some, but now that it was threatened, Oreola realized how much she'd been counting on it.

"Them bankers ain't gonna git everything! I'm a-goin' to Austin to save Ana Maria and El Cid!" Oreola cried, forgetting, in her fervor, her newly acquired grammar. She stood still for a moment, thinking rapidly, part of her hearing Loula Mae running through the house shouting, "Orie is going to Austin!" Then she busied herself, putting a few necessaries and her only change of clothing, a flour sack dress, into an old flour sack. She'd finished packing by the time Ma came hurrying into the room.

"Land sakes, Orie, what's come over you?" she exclaimed.

"Ma, Ana Maria's in trouble and I got to go help her," Oreola tried to explain.

"That little Mexican girl? Well, even if she is, likely as not there's nothing you can do. Show some sense, Orie. Wait till your pa comes home tonight and we'll ask him."

"I can't wait!" cried Oreola, desperately pushing past her bewildered mother. "Wherever the bankers are trying to get their greedy claws on what don't belong to them, that's where I gotta go. Wherever—"

"Orie," her mother interrupted, calling after her, "how you goin' to git to Texas when you ain't got no money?"

As Oreola hurried down the dirt road past the shanties that housed the pickers, she thought hard. There was only one way to get to Austin with no money, and that was by riding the rails. Maybe it was dangerous, but for Ana Maria and El Cid she'd risk anything.

In the train yard, Oreola hesitated, wondering what to do next. There were so many trains—which one would take her to Austin? A voice made her start.

"You lost, dearie?" A stout woman wearing several sweaters over her dress and a pair of men's pants under the skirt stood looking at Oreola with a kindly twinkle in her eye.

"I've got to get to Austin, but I never rode the rails before," Oreola confessed.

"Why, you just follow along of us, and we'll start you on your way," the woman assured her. She turned and gave a whistle and two more hobos slouched out from behind a boxcar. "This here is Peg Leg Al, and this feller goes by the name of Happy Joe," she told Oreola. "You can call me Lady Lou."

"Name's Oreola, but folks call me Orie," said Oreola.

The three hobos exchanged pitying looks. It was bad enough that this girl didn't know a gandy dancer from a stew bum, but to be saddled with such an unimaginative nickname—the trio made an unspoken agreement to help her all they could.

"Well, now," Lady Lou said, putting a protective arm around Oreola, "if it's riding the rails you want to do, I reckon we can teach you a few things."

"First off, you gotta steer clear of the railroad bulls. Them fellers'll throw you off a moving train as soon as look at you and don't I know it," said Peg Leg Al as he gestured toward the source of his name.

"And with you headin' to Austin, why, this is surely your lucky night," offered Happy Joe with a big grin. "The Santa Fe Special is coming through in a few hours and even though it don't stop, it slows way down."

With the trio talking her through the finer points of riding the rails, Oreola became quite adept at hopping on and off the slow-moving freight trains and staying one step ahead of the bulls. Lady Lou, Peg Leg Al, and Happy Joe even shared their food with Oreola, who had only packed a bit of bread soaked in drippings. They passed the long rides across Nevada and Arizona discussing the plight of the worker, FDR, and the fat-cat Eastern bankers.

By the time they crossed the New Mexico border, Oreola had confided in her new friends all about Ana Maria and El Cid and Mr. Pugh and the banker's daughter. When Oreola finished her story, Lady Lou patted her knee kindly and said, "Don't you worry, Orie, me and the boys will make sure you get to Austin on time. I'm sure once this Ana Maria sees you, you won't have to worry about no bankers or their daughters no more."

Oreola smiled weakly. She hoped Lady Lou was right.

At the end of a long week, Oreola and her friends finally made it to Austin. Luckily, Peg Leg Al had spent some time in the city and was able to lead the gang straight to the fairgrounds, although it took all of Oreola's restraint to keep from telling him to move that peg leg of his a little faster. Finally, with her head in a whirl of fear, hope, and anxiety, Oreola spotted corrals full of livestock—the fairgrounds at last!

A young cowhand pointed Oreola to the barrel racing arena—a patch of fenced-in dirt with some stands set up on either side. The stands were crowded with people watching a barrel racer put a painted pony through his paces—doing figure eights around the barrels so rapidly it didn't seem to Oreola that anyone could go faster. Then she caught sight of a beautiful coal-black horse standing in the chute waiting for his turn. A woman held his halter, a sturdy compact woman with a long glossy-black braid down her back. Without thinking, Oreola began to run, and the cry "Ana Maria!" was torn from her throat.

Ana Maria turned and stared, first curiously, then with

growing recognition. She dropped El Cid's halter strap and reached out over the fence rail to take Oreola's outstretched hands. "Oreola, is it really you? I can hardly believe that you are here." When she spoke, her voice was no longer a high, piping little girl's voice, but the rich contralto of a fully developed woman.

"I had to come when I got your letter," said Oreola, patting El Cid's velvety neck as he whinnied happily. "Why did you write that about selling El Cid? What's happened to you, Ana Maria? Don't you want to be a horse trainer no more?"

Ana Maria's eyes filled with tears and she dropped Oreola's hand, turning away as she answered, "My family needs money. I must be practical now."

Oreola bit her lip in frustration. "But what about our plans? Have you forgotten them? What about me? And El Cid?"

Ana Maria looked at her somberly. "No, I have not forgotten. To be a horse trainer was a child's dream. Do you still wish to be a nurse?"

Oreola had to admit that the intervening years had changed her plans as well. "It's true, I have decided that I could better serve the masses as a union organizer," she admitted, but then she added, "but I still always planned on living with you. And El Cid."

Ana Maria looked at Oreola searchingly, but as she opened her mouth to respond, she was interrupted by a shout. "Ana Maria! It's almost your turn!"

Oreola looked up at the girl waving from the stands. She was wearing jodhpurs and a crisp white shirt, and her blond hair was styled in one of those new permanent waves. Oreola felt awash with dislike for the girl. Only the rich could afford permanent waves.

"We will talk more after the race," Ana Maria murmured, mounting El Cid.

"Ana Maria." Oreola put a hand on Ana Maria's polished boot. "If I didn't know religion was an opiate, I'd be praying for you to win."

Ana Maria hesitated a moment. "Oreola . . . I am glad you have come."

Oreola and her hobo friends quickly rushed over and perched themselves on the fence outside the arena. Oreola concentrated all her attention on the black horse and his rider who stood in one corner. A shot rang out and like a whirlwind they were away. Oreola could hardly follow their movements as they flashed around the barrels in a complicated pattern. Then like a streak, they bolted for the finish line. The announcer's voice rang out, "Sixteen point two seconds! Ana Maria Ortiz and El Cid have set a new record for the Texas State Fair Barrel Racing Competition!" Tears of happiness streamed down Oreola's face as her friends whooped and hollered. They all watched Ana Maria standing on El Cid's back, waving her arms for joy as the horse circled the course with a slow, easy canter. Oreola waited until the final two riders took their turns and Ana Maria and El Cid were announced as the winners, then she and her friends went in search of Ana Maria.

In the corral behind the stands, horse and rider were surrounded by a crowd of well-wishers. With a stab of jealousy, Oreola saw that the woman with the permanent wave was standing next to Ana Maria. But when Ana Maria spotted Oreola, she ran to her and embraced her. "We did it, we did it!" she cried. "Just like we planned so many years ago!"

"I knew you could!" Oreola said. "And you too, El Cid! You certainly grew up to be a fine feller!"

As Oreola was petting the horse's nose, the permanent-wave girl joined them and put a proprietary arm around Ana Maria. "Ana Maria," she said, pointedly ignoring Oreola. "Uncle Will is looking for you. He says you can name your price for El Cid."

A shadow fell over Ana Maria's face. "Of course, Katherine. *Momentito.*"

"Ana Maria!" Oreola exclaimed, "You cain't be serious!"

Katherine could ignore Oreola no longer. She turned toward Oreola and asked coldly, "And what business is this of yours?"

Ana Maria hastily intervened. "Katherine, this is my friend Oreola, about whom I have told you . . ." Her voice trailed off as Katherine incredulously looked Oreola up and down.

"So, *this* is the wonderful Oreola?" she asked, curling her lip. Her glance fell on Lady Lou, Peg Leg Al, and Happy Joe standing behind Oreola. "I see you brought the rest of your family," she added cuttingly. Turning to Ana Maria, she said, "When you've finished with old-home week and have made your deal with Uncle Will, come find me. I'll drive us home." She turned and walked away.

Oreola stared at Ana Maria, ignoring the retreating figure and the cries of "Git her! Git her!" and "Kick her in the pants!" erupting from her gang of footloose friends. Ana Maria kept her eyes averted from Oreola as she murmured, "I must go now," then gathered up El Cid's reins and started after Katherine.

Impulsively, Oreola grabbed Ana Maria's arm. "Ana

Maria, is she really what you want? It's not too late for us. We can still make a go of it. You can still get a job as a horse trainer."

Now Ana Maria's eyes filled with tears. "No, Oreola, I can't. I must pay the bank loan and buy Mama's medicine. I must take care of my family. The job at the bank pays twice what any horse-training job would."

"So you're just going to forget about me and go live with Katherine?" Oreola demanded.

Now Ana Maria's eyes were flashing with anger. "You are the one who has made so many new friends in California, and besides that, there are ideological differences between us that I do not think can be reconciled."

"And El Cid?" Oreola asked accusingly.

"Mr. Pugh will pay more than two hundred dollars for El Cid. There is no other way," Ana Maria replied with finality.

Oreola pleaded, "One thing I've learned during these hard times is that you don't sell out your friends and I expect that means you don't sell your friends either. Hasn't El Cid always been a good friend to you?"

"El Cid is a horse. He is livestock. A commodity," replied Ana Maria, her throat catching on the last word.

"It's your kind of thinking that will lead to the workers' uprising," Oreola cried out in frustration.

"It's your kind of thinking that keeps people from working their way to the American Dream," shot back Ana Maria.

"You can can tomatoes, but you can't can the revolution," shouted Oreola, now in an insurrectionist frenzy.

Before Ana Maria could reply, a voice called, "Excuse me, is this where the horse-trading takes place?"

Everyone turned. A woman in a smartly tailored linen

suit was approaching, followed by a florid man wearing tasseled loafers, jodhpurs, a cowboy hat, and a pearl-buttoned shirt.

"I'm Marjorie Rumpelmayer and this is George Steadman. We're here from Oater Studios in Hollywood, California," she said, shaking hands all around.

All the anger drained out of Oreola and Ana Maria. "Hollywood, California!" they repeated in rapturous unison.

"George here will be directing our next picture, *Bandito the Renegade Stallion,*" Marjorie continued efficiently, "and we've been looking everywhere for our Bandito."

"And I'm pleased to say," George continued, "that I think we've found not only our Bandito, but also Little Feather, the Indian princess, and Ellie Buckshot, the barmaid turned outlaw." He beamed at Ana Maria and Oreola.

"But I am Mexican," Ana Maria said, puzzled.

"That doesn't matter," George assured her.

"Say, is there work for us?" asked Lady Lou hopefully. "I can be Chinese if you want."

Marjorie shook her head regretfully, but then stopped as George, eyes closed, put one hand to his head and held the other up in a silencing gesture. Everyone stared at him for a long moment. Then, eyes still shut, he said, "Yes . . . yes . . . I see it! Ellie Buckshot and her ragtag band of happy-go-lucky outlaws, the Patchwork Gang!" George's eyes shot open and he beamed at all of them.

The gang whooped and hollered with delight as Marjorie exclaimed, "Genius! Pure genius! I don't know how you do it, George." George responded with a modest bow.

"In Hollywood, California, do you think that we might

meet Miss Barbara Stanwyck?" Ana Maria timidly ventured.

"After *Bandito* comes out, she'll be asking to meet *you*," Marjorie replied, looking at the attractive girl admiringly.

"Oh, Oreola, I do not want to be a banker. I want to move to Hollywood and live with you and El Cid," Ana Maria said, shedding tears of joy. "I will send money back to my family and I will never, ever forget them."

Oreola flung her arms around her friend. "Ana Maria, how could I have thought that devoting my life to the class struggle would satisfy me when all I ever really wanted was a career in pictures?" As she hugged Ana Maria, George informed her kindly, "You can have a picture career and a little struggle too, if you'd care to join my cell. You won't really understand dialectic materialism until you've heard it explained by Jack Rosenblum, who you may know as Pedro the Singing Bandit."

"Pedro the Singing Bandit is in your cell!" Oreola gasped. "He has the best gol-danged serial I ever seen!"

"Hollywood, here we come!" Lady Lou sang out.

Snake Eyes for Silky

Terry's heart beat in perfect rhythm with the pounding of Silk Stockings's hooves on the dirt track. The ride was so effortless that they were flying down the home stretch before Terry realized that the race was almost over and they were ahead of the field. The sweat turned to ice on the wiry jockey's back as she began to pull up on Silky's reins. Her eyes flicked over to the grandstand, which revealed nothing more than peeling paint and a small weekday crowd of men who were as rundown as the faded racetrack. After seconds that felt like days, a rangy bay came up on the outside, beating Silk Stockings by a nose. Terry felt a surge of relief. She knew that slipping up was as good as making a date with a dark alley and a couple of thugs who'd use her as a dance floor.

Terry tried to savor the feeling of relief like it was a lover's last kiss, but kisses soon fade and Terry felt the familiar flood of bitterness wash away the relief. Terry knew that Silky was the one—a horse with the kind of speed and heart that every jockey dreams about. When Shorty, Silky's trainer, had offered her a steady job riding the chestnut filly a year ago she could hardly believe it. With all the boys back from the war, jockeys were a dime a dozen, and a woman had a better shot at picking the trifecta in a twenty-horse race than she did of getting work as a jockey. Terry had been scraping by as a training rider, a groom, even mucking stalls. She'd wondered why Shorty picked her for the job, and when she'd heard the owner's name, Ginger Delmonico, Terry figured it must be a hand-up from the woman owner, another gal trying to make it in the rough-and-tumble world of racing. With a steady job riding a promising horse, Terry had felt like she was holding a hand full of aces until just before her first race when Shorty told her how things would be.

"Listen, doll, dese are the rules. When the word comes down to lose, dis horse gotta lose. I don't make dese rules, but I see you got a pretty face there and maybe you wanna keep it dat way, so if I was you, when the word comes down, well, dat's what I'd do."

Terry had been around the track long enough to know the score and she'd always tried to fly right, but that day Terry found out that right and wrong could get awfully tangled up inside an empty stomach. She'd thought again about Ginger Delmonico, and laughed bitterly. Some helping hand! This Delmonico dame must be one shrewd sister, and cold, figuring a lady jockey wouldn't have many places to go if she didn't like the dirty hand she was dealt.

Terry had decided it would be a one-shot deal—after the race was over, she'd kiss this horse goodbye. But she hadn't counted on Silky and what it felt like to be on her back when she was running like the wind. By the end of that first race, she knew she was stuck with this horse for the long haul. But she made a promise—a promise to herself and to Silky that someday Silky would get her chance.

Now as Terry walked back and forth, cooling Silky down after the race, she thought about her vow. The months had flown by and Silky was readier than ever to be a champ. Terry paused a moment to admire her, the high withers, the sloping shoulders, the muscles of her powerful hindquarters rippling under her glossy chestnut coat. If only they could get out of this second-rate track and find a race the mob didn't have its finger in! Terry scowled at the ground. Who was she kidding? It was Ginger Delmonico who held the whip, and Ginger wasn't thinking about anything but quick money. Without Ginger's say-so, Silky would never have a chance to show her stuff. Terry's head ached with thinking. All she wanted now was couple of quick ones at Gillespie's to dull the pain of betraying Silky yet again. Lately that was becoming a habit after each race. Maybe one day she'd forget her vow altogether . . .

As Terry was stabling Silky, Shorty leaned into the stall and said with a leer, "Miz Delmonico wants a word wit' you." Outside, Ginger Delmonico was sitting in her shiny new Phantom Arrow, the set of her mouth getting tighter with each cloud of cigarette smoke she exhaled. This was only the second time she'd asked to see Terry. That first time Ginger had done little more than cock her head, letting cigarette smoke trail from her flared nostrils and murmur, "Well, what do you know," a faint note of surprise in her voice. For her part, Terry had summed her up as a seasoned filly with nice conformation, good action, dark red hair a shade lighter than Silky's, and just as carefully groomed. How had she acquired Silk Stockings, and what had drawn her into this dirty racket? But there was no time to puzzle over that now. Ginger had caught sight of her, and was impatiently beckoning her over.

"I don't know who you think you are, but you'd do well to remember that you work for me and nobody makes a fool of Ginger Delmonico," she said rapidly. "You and I both know that you were lucky back there on the track. You've never given me any trouble, but make no mistake, one slipup"—Ginger paused, narrowed her eyes, and leaned in so close that Terry could feel the heat of the other woman's breath on her own face—"let's just say that the stables can be an awfully dangerous place for a little thing like you."

"I haven't slipped up, and I won't," Terry quickly shot back.

But Ginger wasn't done. "I'm surprised you could even get that kind of a stride out of the old nag," she said with a sneering laugh.

"That shows what you know! Silky could be a champion, if you'd only wise up and let her!" The rash words were out of Terry's mouth before she had a chance to stop herself.

Ginger's eyes widened momentarily in surprise. Then she quickly spit out, "Make tracks, before I decide to get angry." Terry didn't need to be told twice. She turned toward Gillespie's as she heard the Phantom, with a clashing of gears, roar off behind her.

Everybody at Gillespie's was buzzing about Sailor's Delight, the horse who'd beaten Silky, as Terry slid onto a stool at the bar. "Gimme a double," Terry ordered, and tried to close her ears to the chatter around her. "He's only run two races as a three-year-old, but he's got quite a reputation—a second Man O' War!" "Five'll get you ten he's a cinch for the Bluegrass Stakes."

"Another," said Terry to the bartender. She didn't want to listen to any more talk about Sailor's Delight. She knew that all this buzz should have been about Silky—they should have been saying that Silky was the next big champion. As if in answer to her thoughts, she heard someone ask, "What about Silk Stockings? She sure gave Sailor's Delight a run for his money." A veteran handicapper snorted his answer. "Okay to show or place, maybe, but she doesn't have a winner's heart." Terry knocked back her second double and stumbled out of the bar, a dull pain that had nothing to do with whiskey clouding her vision.

The morning before the next race, Terry fed Silky herself—making up the bran mash just the way the filly liked it. She crooned, "You can do it, girl," and "This one's in the bag," into Silky's ear. Silky nickered, tossed her head, and pawed the ground as if to tell Terry she was ready to beat all comers. Just before Terry led Silky to the starting gate, Shorty showed up. "The word's come down—pull up lame," he muttered. Before Terry could stop him, he pulled out a small knife, bent down, and swiftly nicked Silky's right front fetlock. The truth Terry'd been hiding from all day hit her like a grand piano dropped from a seventh-story window.

The fetlock would heal in a week, Terry knew, but what about the risk to Silky, running full speed on a weakened leg? Terry was sick with fear as Silky shot out of the starting gate.

As they headed toward the third rail, her fears were realized—she felt Silky's rhythmic stride falter. She tried to slow the filly, but gamely the horse pressed on, until suddenly she stumbled, and went down on her knees. After a heart-stopping moment, the horse struggled to her feet, and limped to the finish line.

Instantly, Terry was off Silky's back, and bending over her forelegs, cursing herself. Silky wasn't really hurt, but that was no consolation. Terry had known the risks and she'd run the race anyway. Bitterly, she realized that she was no better than Shorty and his scalpel.

As she straightened up, a voice from the stands floated down and caught her ear, "I told you that filly just ain't got the heart—or the legs." The words flicked Terry on the raw, and there was no whiskey in her to cushion the pain. She managed to toss the reins to Shorty and find a spot behind the stables where no one would see her. Terry was punching the stable wall, choking back sobs, when she realized that she was not alone.

"I thought you were made of tougher stuff than this with the lip you laid on me after the last race," said a familiar husky voice.

Ginger's taunt turned all of Terry's tears into pure fight as she turned to face Silky's nemesis. "What would you know about tough? You think being tough is about pushing people around that can't do nothing about it? That ain't tough. That's just cheap. You ever think maybe it's caring about something that makes you tough? Well, I care about Silky and I can't stand to do wrong by her no more! So go ahead—do me in! Do it right now!"

Ginger reached inside her purse and then paused, her face enigmatic, her eyes on Terry's. Terry held her breath—was this how it would end? Here, in this dirty spot behind a racetrack? She closed her eyes. But instead of a bullet, she felt Ginger grasp her arms. The big redhead pulled Terry close and kissed her roughly, then gently, then roughly again. Before Terry had a chance to think about what was happening, she felt the cold steel of a gun pressing into her side, and Ginger, a cigarette clenched between her teeth, was hissing, "Step lively, sister, we're going to my place."

Terry's thoughts were moving faster than the Phantom, which roared along with Terry at the wheel and Ginger seated menacingly, yet seductively, beside her. Escape—but where to? Terry's whole world was the track. And if she stayed in that world, Ginger would always be able to find her. But did she really want to escape? Silky meant the world to Terry, but a girl has some needs that even the best horse can't satisfy. A dame like Ginger Delmonico could satisfy those needs and then some.

When they got to Ginger's place, a suite of rooms in a quietly luxurious hotel off Lake Shore Drive, Terry still didn't know how this visit was going to play out. Terry took in the living room, from the gold and crystal bar to the white leather sofa to the cream-colored carpeting—it looked like money. Ginger poured herself a drink at the bar, then stood sipping it, sizing Terry up. She still held her gun, but loosely, almost as if she'd forgotten about it. Terry stared back, still in her racing silks soaked with sweat, her dusty boots sinking into the plush carpet. Finally Ginger spoke.

"So what do you think I should do with you for mouthing off to me like that?"

Terry decided to play it a little dangerous. "Maybe you should teach me a lesson I won't forget."

"Oh, so you think you're ready to play with the grown-ups now, do you?"

"Who says I'm playing?"

"I say. I say when you're playing and when you're not. Maybe you forgot who owns you?"

Again Ginger's words made Terry forget any danger in her desire to show Ginger once and for all that nobody owned her. Without thinking, she covered the ground between them and grasped the ends of the long silk scarf that hung around Ginger's neck as if she were going to rein in an unruly horse. She thought about tightening the scarf until Ginger begged for mercy, but instead she found herself tugging on it just enough to bring Ginger's mouth to hers. Then they were in the bedroom, and Terry showed Ginger that Silky wasn't the only one she could get to the finish line. Afterward, Ginger looked younger, almost vulnerable, as she lay back in the bed, her red hair tousled on the cream satin pillow. Terry's eyes traveled from Ginger's red hair to the white and gold painted vanity, where the small snub-nosed revolver lay forgotten. Ginger didn't need threats to keep Terry around; they both knew that now.

"Penny for your thoughts," said Ginger with a voluptuous smile.

"You're stabled pretty nice here, and I can see you've got no worries about where your next bucket of oats is coming from, so why do you need to make Silk Stockings a loser?"

The small jockey nearly fell off the bed as Ginger jerked upright, not bothering to cover her heaving bosom.

"That horse is my business!" she hissed. "You're just the hired hand! You got that, sister?"

Terry got out of the bed and began to pull on her silks. The horsy smell on them was like a breath of fresh air, reminding her of her promise to Silky. Terry reached for her boots.

"What's your hurry, Terry?" Ginger's voice was casual, seductive, as if she regretted spoiling the party.

"I've got work to do at the stables—Silky needs me." Terry continued to pull on her boots.

Ginger leaned over and took a cigarette out of the gold box next to the revolver, and lit it with a crystal lighter. She blew out a cloud of gray-blue smoke, looking at Terry through half-closed eyes. "Go ahead, sweetheart, go to your horse. You'll be back." Her mocking laughter seemed to follow Terry out the door, through the hotel lobby, and even on the long ride home on the Elevated.

It was like Ginger said. As much as she fought it, Terry found herself in that white and gold suite after almost every race. She felt split in two as she bounced between Silky's back and Ginger's bed. Race after race went by and each time word would come down from the boss to finish in the money, out of the money, pull up lame—whatever was needed so that the right people would go home happy. And afterward the gleaming Phantom Arrow would be waiting for Terry. Terry could feel Shorty's beady eyes watching her as she got in. He said nothing, just leered more than ever as he gave her instructions for each race. The orders always came down through Shorty—Terry and Ginger never talked about Silky or anything to do with horses or the track. Sometimes they never talked at all. When Terry slid her hand under Ginger's silver fox furs and found flesh as soft as Silky's muzzle, she felt like this thing between her and Ginger was enough. But when she was with Silky, a voice inside her head told her this couldn't last, shouldn't last. Terry didn't want to listen to it.

Then one day there was no word from Shorty before the race. When Terry spurred Silky on to the track, she realized with a sudden jolt that she could run this race the way she wanted. It was only a cheap claiming race, but Terry and Silky ran as if it were the Kentucky Derby, leaving the second-place horse behind by twenty lengths. Afterward, Terry hailed a cab, too impatient to wait for the Phantom

Arrow. She had to see Ginger right away. Ginger had to know how Terry dreamed of winning. Was this her way of giving in? Was she starting to care about Terry?

Terry flew up the stairs to Ginger's suite, a box of roses under her arm. Her hand was on the doorknob when she heard voices inside.

"I told you, I didn't have time to get to Shorty!" Ginger's voice had a pleading tone that Terry had never heard before.

"I dunno what Ginger's story is here, but you know you can count on me, Jimmy—I didn't hear nothing, so I didn't do nothing. Me, I just do what I'm told."

Terry recognized Shorty's familiar whine, but the next voice was unfamiliar.

"Save the excuses, old man—that damn horse won by twenty lengths—you know what that does to the odds?"

Ginger was talking again. "Maybe we could figure a way to work these odds in our favor."

There was silence for a moment and then the stranger spoke again. "You trying to tell me how to run my business, honey?"

"No, Jimmy, you got me all wrong. I know who calls the shots." Terry almost didn't recognize Ginger's voice, she sounded so subdued.

"All right doll, just so you don't forget." The menace in the stranger's voice was unmistakable.

"Yeah, Jimmy, you're the one with the brains. Everybody knows that. My girl here screws up again, I'll be the first to let you know. You can count on that, Jimmy."

"My girl?" Terry wondered.

The voices had been coming closer, and Terry managed to slip behind the door just as it opened. Through the crack between the door and wall she caught a glimpse of this Jimmy, a big man, well dressed and genial-looking, except for his small hard eyes. "You're looking good these days, doll," he said, reaching up to grasp Ginger's chin and turn her head from side to side. "Am I still your best fella?"

"Of course, Jimmy."

Jimmy gave a humorless laugh as he released Ginger's face, then turned and headed down to the waiting elevator, Shorty shuffling behind him. Ginger stood in the doorway, watching them until the elevator had closed, and then she went back inside, closing the door. Terry was alone in the hallway again.

Terry felt like she'd been punched in the stomach half a dozen times, or maybe it was more like Silky had up and kicked her in the head. The blinkers were off now—she was just a little side dish to keep Ginger amused when Jimmy wasn't around, and Silky's win had been a mistake. She and Silky were no closer to their goal than they'd been before.

Terry drew a deep breath. The time had come to be true to Silky. She might as well finish with that two-timing dame now.

When Terry opened the door, Ginger was sitting on the edge of her white leather divan, her face pale, her eyes staring at nothing. Her gloves and hat were on the white leather love seat, as if she'd just come in and thrown them there. She turned quickly at the sound of the door, her hand going automatically to her purse. When she saw Terry, she relaxed a little.

"Well, look what the cat dragged in. I didn't send the car for you."

"I came on my own two feet."

"What do you know, you got your own transportation.

Drink?" As Ginger got up, Terry's eyes were drawn to the gray tailor-made and she couldn't help noticing the way it showed off Ginger's figure.

"Sure." Terry slumped into a chair.

Ginger poured a Scotch—double, just the way Terry liked it—and handed it to her. "What's in the box?"

Terry had forgotten about the roses she carried under her arm. She looked down at them. "I got roses," she said. "To celebrate winning the race. Silky came in first, just like I knew she could."

"Yeah, I heard," said Ginger. "Sorry, honey, but I wouldn't count on too many more of those."

"Skip the song and dance, Ginger, I know the score," said Terry, suddenly boiling mad.

Ginger looked surprised. "What do you mean, you know the score? What score do you think you know?"

"I heard you in here with your boyfriend Jimmy," said Terry. Ginger set her drink down hard, an exclamation on her lips. "Save it, Ginger," said Terry. "You've been using me, yeah, and two-timing me for a while, but the ride's over now. I'm getting out of this racket."

"Why, you two-bit jockey, you think you're walking out on Ginger Delmonico? After all I've done for you?" Ginger was white with fury.

"Sure you've done a lot for me," jeered Terry, all the bitterness inside her pouring out. "I guess I should be grateful a dame like you would even give me the time of day. What else have I got the right to expect—me, the daughter of a drunk who took off before I was fourteen, no brains, no education, no good for anything or anybody, just a sawed-off runt who's got a way with horses. Thanks, lady, but no thanks to your dirty job, and your dirty racket!"

Ginger grabbed Terry's arm as she turned to leave. "You

think it was an accident, you winning today? You think I won't pay for that pretty trophy you won?"

"Wh-what are you talking about?" Terry stuttered.

"You think Jimmy is my boyfriend? I got news for you, sister—he's my ex-husband. Maybe you've heard of Jimmy "Snake Eyes" Galanti?"

Terry gasped. Jimmy "Snake Eyes" Galanti had his finger in every gambling racket in Cook County.

"Silk Stockings is what you might call alimony," Ginger continued. "Or maybe it's just Jimmy's way of making sure he'll always have his hooks in me. Sure, I was married," she said in answer to Terry's shocked look.

"Your old man left you high and dry?" Ginger went on. "You should count yourself lucky. My old man never had any use for me until I found my way into a little of the green stuff and he hasn't stopped trying to farm my cabbage patch ever since. Yeah, that Shorty, he's some kinda father."

"Shorty!" gasped Terry.

"Yeah, Shorty. So don't come crying to me about lousy fathers. You bet I married Jimmy. Growing up in my neighborhood, there was only one way out for a girl and that was to find some joe who had what it took and hitch along for the ride. Jimmy was the guy with all the angles and that made him the guy I wanted. Of course, I had my angle and it was a doozy, but I figured if Jimmy didn't know it was the dames I went for, well, it wouldn't hurt him any."

"Haven't you ever been square with anybody?" Terry couldn't help asking.

Ginger stopped pacing and glared at her. "What'd you want me to do? The only way loving some broad was gonna get me out of that neighborhood was if it bought me a trip to the state pen. Besides, I don't see you being any kind of saint. I think you know as well as the next gal how to do what you gotta do and maybe what you gotta do is different from what I did but that don't make you any better."

Terry bit her lip. Ginger was right about that!

"So Jimmy does a guy a favor and goes to Joliet for a couple years. Then the guy collects on some favors from a judge he knows and Jimmy's out on parole. He thinks he's going to surprise me." Ginger gave a short, humorless laugh. "Well, we were both surprised. He finds me in bed with a girl, and to make it worse, this particular tomato is an old friend of Jimmy's, if you know what I mean. He slaps me around pretty good, and tosses me out. A couple weeks later I get the ownership papers for Silk Stockings in the mail. He needed an owner with a clean bill of health, and everybody knows Jimmy's got a record longer than the racing sheet. And then Shorty shows up to keep an eye on me. Try telling him blood's thicker than water and see how hard he'll laugh."

Ginger paused to take a breath, and when she spoke again, her voice had a sobbing sound, like a violin at a Hungarian restaurant.

"So here I've been, trying to stash away enough to clear out, and then you come along with your crazy dreams and your heart in your eyes, and those strong, gentle hands—" Ginger stopped herself, biting her lip.

Terry sat there, her head in a whirl! It was all so confusing—Jimmy was Ginger's ex-husband! Shorty was her father! Then Ginger's mother must have been the tall one, Terry thought, trying to piece it all together. She stared at Ginger, who was tossing back another drink. Terry's head ached, as if someone had spent the evening pounding on it with a ballpeen hammer. Ginger poured herself a third drink, and knocked it back. There was something Terry's brain was trying to tell her, something about Silky and the spirited way she tossed her head right before a race. Silky—Ginger—Ginger—Silky—When Terry stared at Ginger, it seemed as if the horse was in the room with them, pawing the cream-colored carpet.

"What are you looking at?" Ginger demanded crossly.

Suddenly it all came together, like a starting bell going off in her brain, and Terry almost laughed out loud. She was all done with being torn in two! She didn't have to choose between Silky and Ginger—the path to the finish line was the same for both these fillies! Both of them were being ridden into the ground by Jimmy, and it was up to Terry to knock him off their backs. And she thought that maybe she had the plan to do it.

"Listen," she said eagerly, her words tumbling over each other. "Today at the stables everybody was talking about the Bluegrass Stakes, and how Sailor's Delight is going to be running. All we gotta do is get Silky into that race and we're home free!"

"What?" Ginger was confused, but she saw that Terry wasn't walking out so she kept talking. "You've got a one-horse mind, kid. I've just finished telling you that Silky isn't going to get any more chances to win. Jimmy's in the saddle, *capisce?*"

"But this isn't just any other race! When Silky wins the Bluegrass, she'll be so famous, Jimmy and his gang won't be able to touch her! Or you!"

Terry saw a faint hope growing in Ginger's eyes, but she had to play it tough. She was that kind of dame.

"Did that nag kick you in the head or something? How's she going to win the Bluegrass Stakes? Now don't get sore—I know you think this filly is fast, but she's never run in a race that's more than bush league and now you think she's going to win the biggest race of 'em all?"

"She's raced against Sailor's Delight. He's going to run the Bluegrass and Silky could have beat him."

"Slow down, kid. I know all about Sailor's Delight, and yeah, you got it right that he's going to run, but even he isn't in the same league. I got the inside dope and that horse won't go off at less than thirty-five to one."

Terry knew that Ginger was looking at this thing the smart way. Right now, at least she and Ginger were alive with all their parts in working order. If they entered that race and lost, that would all change pretty quick. Ginger was smart, but Terry knew something that Ginger didn't. Terry knew that there wasn't any race anywhere that Silky couldn't win. She grasped Ginger's arms, looking intently into her eyes.

"Your job is to get Silky into the race. My job is to win it. I know I can do my job. Can you do yours?"

A challenge was never wasted on Ginger Delmonico. She knew a few people who would do a favor for her and keep it quiet, and she went about securing a spot in the biggest event in horse racing for a filly who'd won only a few small-time races at a small-time track. It wasn't easy and it wasn't cheap. Terry realized that one day when she went up to Ginger's suite. Something was missing. "Your gold and crystal bar!" she exclaimed.

"I hocked it," said Ginger. "I was drinking too much anyway." Terry went to Ginger's closet and opened it. "And your silver fox furs!" she lamented.

"Don't worry, baby," Ginger hastened to console her. "Look what I got in exchange." She pulled out a cardboard dress box. "Go ahead, open it," she urged.

Terry opened the box, revealing brand new racing silks in white and gold. "They're perfect!" she exclaimed with pleasure.

"Think of us here, when you ride Silky," Ginger murmured suggestively.

Terry looked with pride at Ginger. That once hardnosed filly was gentled, and Terry rewarded her the way she rewarded all her horses—with a little sugar. Later, as the evening shadows crept their way up the cream satin sheets, Terry said, "You never stop surprising me, Ginger."

"I have one more surprise for you," said Ginger. She led Terry over to the window, and there, where the Phantom Arrow was usually parked, was a gold horse van. "I figured you'd want Silky to travel in style."

Terry was on cloud nine as she prepared Silky for the Stakes, but she had to keep reminding herself that they weren't out of the woods yet. All of Silky's extra training had to be done in the dead of night, after Shorty had left the track. He was the worm in the apple. Silky grew fitter than ever, and Terry prayed that the race would come before Shorty wised up. It was getting harder and harder to convince the filly to lose when each night she was being asked to run like a champion. But luck was on their side, and at last only one hurdle remained—getting Silky to the Stakes.

Every horse running in the Bluegrass Stakes was being brought in at least a week before the race, but a week would be more than enough time for Shorty to notice that Silky was missing and tip off Jimmy. The evening before the Bluegrass Stakes, Terry was grooming Silky, waiting for Ginger to arrive with the van. Her mind was wrapped up in dreams of her and Ginger and a little house with a white and gold picket fence and acres of open pasture for Silky. She started slightly when she heard Shorty's whine.

"Dat horse is sure lookin' good," he said. Shorty was leaning over the stall door, chewing on an old stogie. Terry bit her lip in vexation. Damn that old man!

"Yup," continued Shorty conversationally, "she sure has got a glow." He leered at Terry. "Miz Delmonico, she got a kind of a glow too, don't she?"

Terry had to get rid of Shorty fast, before Ginger arrived with the van!

She pushed back her disgust and turned to Shorty.

"Silky is looking good, isn't she? You must be putting something special in her oats." Terry forced a smile. "Here, old-timer"—she dug in her pocket for a silver dollar—"reward for a job well done."

The old man's rheumy eyes lit up as he caught the coin Terry tossed to him, and he shuffled out of the barn in the direction of Gillespie's.

Terry sighed with relief as she caught sight of the gold van pulling up outside the barn. She decided not to tell Ginger about her conversation with Shorty. There was no point in worrying her now—especially since she had to drive the whole 500 miles to the Bluegrass herself. Terry was riding in the back with Silky. She knew Ginger needed her, but Silky needed her more. With a hasty kiss to Ginger, she loaded Silky into the van and settled down next to her. Silky whinnied excitedly as the truck's engine roared to life. "Don't worry, girl," Terry soothed her, "you're finally gonna get your chance!"

They pulled in at the track at ten in the morning, Ginger's face white with fatigue and Terry stiff and cramped from the close quarters. But Silky was calm and fresh, and that was what mattered. The start time was 2 P.M. sharp. Terry groomed Silky and warmed her up, while

Ginger stood nearby, smoking cigarette after cigarette. Terry wondered what she was thinking as they both watched the competition—sleek, tautly muscled horses being pampered by teams of well-trained professionals. These were horses that were used to winning, horses that had been bred to win. But Terry knew that all those fancy sires weren't worth a damn—Silky had the speed and that was what counted. But did she have the will to win after being made to lose for so long? They'd find out soon enough.

"You'd better get ready," Ginger said, dropping her cigarette and grinding it under her heel. As Terry and Silky followed Ginger, Terry spotted a man leaning against the side of the gold van. She'd seen him only once, but she'd never forget those snakelike eyes. He straightened up as Ginger approached, and she stopped in her tracks. "Jimmy!" she exclaimed.

"Hi, doll," said Jimmy, peering at Ginger. "Well, Shorty told me something was up, but I doubt he would have pictured this—Silk Stockings at the Bluegrass Stakes!" A rumbling laugh shook him.

"What do you want, Jimmy?" The voice was expressionless, but Terry could tell from Ginger's rigid back there was a cocktail of fear and anger mixing inside her.

"What do I want?" Jimmy looked at the sky as if it held the answer to the question. "Me, all I wanted was to share some good news with you. Now that this filly of yours is running in the big time, I figured you should have some protection. So I had her insured for a million bucks." He paused for a moment, but no one said anything.

"Don't get me wrong—it'd be a real shame if something happened to her, but a horse like this, trying to run a race that's out of her league, could end up with a broken leg." Jimmy shrugged his shoulders and smiled as he continued, "Happens all the time."

A cold sweat began to drip down Terry's back. Silky, her leg broken—probably Shorty would be the one to take her out and put a bullet in her brain.

"And I'm not going to be selfish about the money—share and share alike, that's me," Jimmy continued, his eyes never leaving Ginger. "There'll be enough to pension the old man off—I know you never liked him, and truth to tell, I'm getting a little sick of him myself. It'll be just like old times, huh, Ginger? There's worse things than a million bucks, right, doll?"

Terry's hand tightened on Silky's halter. What would Ginger say? A million bucks was the kind of dough that could turn someone's feelings on their head. And Jimmy was playing her like a piano with his smooth talk. Terry could do nothing but wait, helplessly.

Ginger was answering Jimmy, her voice dull, "S-sure Jimmy, I guess there's worse things. Maybe, though, there could be some other way for you to—" Suddenly she threw her head up as if she'd heard the starting bell. "Put those down!"

Jimmy had picked up the new white and gold racing silks and was casually running his hand over them. He looked startled at Ginger's sudden change of temperament. "Listen," he began menacingly, but Ginger didn't let him finish.

"I don't want your dirty hands touching anything of mine ever again," she said in a low, thrilling tone. "You can do what you like to me, but Silky's going to run this race and she's going to win it!"

Terry felt a rush of pride flow through her at Ginger's

defiance. Jimmy stared at her for a second, and then let out a huge belly laugh.

"Win! You actually think this nag is going to win! I never thought I'd see the day Ginger Delmonico would turn sucker. Don't you know what the odds are? Two hundred to one!"

"I know the odds," said Ginger.

Jimmy whooped some more. "Ginger Delmonico, betting a hopeless long shot, with a sure thing staring her in the face!" His smile twisted contemptuously. "You sure must be soft on this little jockey."

"Leave her out of this!" The words tore out of Ginger as if someone had put a hot branding iron on her thigh.

Jimmy continued to smile, but in a way that sent chills down Terry's spine. "Tell you what, Ginger. I'll let this one race go. Let's make a bet on it. If Silk Stockings wins, she's yours, no more strings attached. But if by some strange chance, she loses . . ." Now even the smile was gone.

"If she loses?" prompted Ginger in a voice Terry could barely recognize.

"The jockey's out, I'm in, and the horse is dead," said Jimmy. And now his voice was like ice. "But you already knew that, didn't you, doll?"

"It's a bet," said Ginger. Jimmy put out his hand and Ginger took it as if it were a coiled snake.

"I'll see you after the race." Jimmy's parting words hit Terry like a fist in the gut.

Ginger staggered, almost collapsing against the van after he'd left. Terry dropped Silky's halter and ran to her side. "Ginger!" she cried, tears springing to her eyes.

"Can that sob stuff, sister," Ginger croaked weakly, "you've get a race to run. Get these silks on, it's time to weigh in."

"What about you?" Terry said anxiously. Ginger looked as drained of blood as if she were a steer who'd just taken a trip to the stockyards.

"Don't you worry about me." Ginger summoned up a weak smile. "Ginger Delmonico always lands on her feet."

Terry knew it was all up to Silky now. Would she and Ginger have a life together, or would Ginger be forced back into the mob, forced to endure the caresses of the man who'd beaten her, kicked her out on the street, and killed her horse? Would Terry go back to the occasional exhibition race, the whiskies at Gillespie's? Would she end up a drunk, like her old man, her days spent shoveling manure to earn the price of a bottle, her nights in some alley, with the Elevated rumbling overhead? And Silky—what would be her measure of pain and suffering? What would be her last thoughts before Shorty put a bullet through her brain? Terry couldn't even let herself think about that. She buried her face in Silky's neck for a brief moment before she swung astride her and headed for the track.

Terry felt like she was in a dream as the starting crew got the horses to the gate. The starter raised his pistol and the crowd fell quiet. There was the shot, the gate opened, and with that proud toss of her head, Silky was off!

The roar of the crowd and the pounding of horses' hooves blurred together in Terry's ears. Ginger's face, pale and pinched, floated before her, then Jimmy's with his hard eyes and Shorty's with his leer, then Silky's long horsy face with a quizzical expression. Suddenly the faces disappeared like so many popped balloons. She was in the Bluegrass Stakes and Silky was running the race of her life!

After two furlongs, Silky was one of four horses in the lead, four horses running so closely together you couldn't see daylight between them. Bottoms Up, the favorite, was hugging the rail, with Sailor's Delight, Silky, and Southern Comfort in a huddle next to him. As they rounded the turn after the fourth furlong, Southern Comfort began to fade back. At the same time, Bottoms Up lengthened his stride on the stretch, so that he led by half a length, while Sailor's Delight and Silky ran neck and neck. Terry felt a growing confidence and excitement—she knew that Silky still had speed to burn.

Suddenly, as they rounded the second turn, Terry noticed something—as Sailor's Delight faded back, so did Silky. What was wrong? Had the night in the van been too much for her? Or was it—and now Terry's heart caught in her throat—was it that Silky remembered that she was supposed to lose to Sailor's Delight? Terry felt sick inside—not just at what losing now would mean, but at the thought that she had turned Silky into a horse without heart—what everybody had believed her to be all along.

Terry leaned forward and whispered fiercely into Silky's ear, "I never gave up on you, Silky! Don't you dare give up on yourself!" Silky's ears twitched, intelligently. Terry loosened the reins and Silky leaned forward, as if testing her freedom. Slowly, she gained on Sailor's Delight and passed him. Bottoms Up was now two lengths ahead. Then one length. Now Silky's nose was even with Bottoms Up's withers. They were coming into the final stretch. The crowd was cheering madly, but Terry didn't even hear them. Again Bottoms Up lengthened his stride, but Silky went one better—she flew across the finish line.

The colors of the track blurred and ran together in Terry's eyes, like a watercolor painting left out in the rain. As she brought Silky down to a canter, the crowd began to pour onto the track, past the track police, who were helpless to stop them. They had just witnessed the biggest upset of the century, and they wanted to get as close as they could to the horse who'd done it. Through the roar of the crowd the loudspeakers blared the voice of the track announcer, making the win official. "And by a nose, Silk Stockings beats the favorite, Bottoms Up, to win the Bluegrass Stakes!" Now Silky's name would be on everyone's lips.

Terry turned Silky around and headed toward the winner's circle, her eyes anxiously searching the stands for a redhead in a white and gold dress. Where was Ginger?

Suddenly she saw her, not in the stands, but on the track hurrying toward her, trailing photographers, reporters, and track officials behind her. When they met in the middle of the track, Terry slid off Silky into Ginger's tight embrace. Over Ginger's shoulder, Terry saw Jimmy, his face purple with rage, trying to reach them, but he was pushed aside by a photographer, and the flashbulbs began to pop.

Ginger handed her a ticket as the crowd began pushing them toward the winner's circle.

"What's this?" Terry asked, beginning to smile.

"I put our last hundred dollars on Silk Stockings to win—do you think I did the right thing?" Ginger asked with a sly grin.

"I hear it's a sucker bet," Terry teased her.

"Love is always a sucker bet," said Ginger. "This time I decided to be one of the suckers."

The Chosen Horse

Lena hurried along the narrow, tenement-lined streets. Her brown eyes darted everywhere and her nose quivered at each new smell wafting past, but she knew that today she must not allow herself to be distracted. Mama had told her to go to the market, buy the pickles, and come straight home, but Lena had decided that if she ran the whole way there and back, there would be time for a visit with her two friends.

Still, when she spotted Izzy, the pool hall owner, handing a thick roll of bills to Officer O'Brien, she could not repress her curiosity. "Why are you giving money to Officer O'Brien? Does he work at the pool hall when he is not being a policeman?" Lena jumped back just in time to avoid the billy club that the normally good-natured policeman swiped in her direction.

Lena hurried on, but spotted another acquaintance farther up the street—Guido, the organ grinder, with his monkey Pepe. As she approached them, Lena shouted out,

"How's business, Guido? Have you had more visits from . . . what did you call them . . . the Cosa Nostra?" Guido scolded her in rapid Italian, crossing himself. Lena sighed and continued on her way. How she wished she understood Italian!

Lena knew that she should keep her questions to herself—Mama and Papa had been telling her this since she was a little girl. In the neighborhood they called her "Lena of the thousand questions," and laughed at her everlasting curiosity. Still, Lena's thirst for knowledge was so great, that questions seemed to rise unbidden from her lips. Her greatest sorrow in life had always been that, because she was a girl, the study of the Talmud, which contained the greatest wisdom of her people, was forbidden to her. Lena quickened her pace as she thought of how that sorrow had been replaced by joy since she met her two friends.

"Ooof!" Lena's thoughts were so busy, she had tripped over the wizened old Pretzel Woman, who always sat on a little stool, her basket of pretzels beside her, at the corner of Essex and Delancey. She was wrapped in so many shawls it was hard to tell whether she was a person or a pile of dry goods.

"Ho, little maid," said the Pretzel Woman in her high, cracked voice. "Where are you going, and in such a hurry? Why are you not at home, helping your mama prepare for the Sabbath?"

"I—I'm on my way," Lena said guiltily, thinking about Mama waiting at home for her pickles. "Please, Pretzel Woman, can you tell me where Johnny Apple is?"

The Pretzel Woman raised an eyebrow at Lena and answered in her usual cryptic fashion, "Where is a horse when he is bidden to do the work of man, and man is driven by the will of God, but still must live in the world among men, as must a horse, if the nature of the horse is to be that which God intended?"

Of course! Lena's keen mind soon unraveled the old woman's puzzle—Johnny would be on the corner of Orchard Street, where the crowds were thickest! "Thank you, Pretzel Woman," Lena called as she hastened away.

Lena knew people thought it odd that her best friend was a horse, but Johnny Apple wasn't just any horse, although most people didn't give him a second glance. He hardly came up to the chest of the huge draft horses that pulled the beer carts and he wasn't fast or sleek like the police horses that broke up the union riots. He was a practical horse, small but sturdy, with a thick, rough coat that served him well during the harsh New York winters, when he stood for hours hitched to Mr. Karpels's fruit cart. There was nothing extraordinary about Johnny Apple's size or beauty, but this unassuming little cart horse possessed a wisdom beyond other horses—even a wisdom beyond many people.

The first time Lena had seen Johnny Apple, she had been toting a heavy basket of laundry to deliver to Mrs. Santucci, who ran a boarding house on the Bowery. Lena's mama took in washing to make ends meet, and it was Lena's job to deliver the clean laundry. That day, Johnny Apple was standing patiently while Mr. Karpels bargained with a housewife over the price of a pound of apples. Lena had petted his velvety nose, and he had blown his sweet horse breath over the laundry basket. When she picked up her basket to trudge wearily on, quick as a wink, the horse had turned his head to snatch an apple from the cart and tossed it so that it landed smack in the middle of the clean folded sheets. Lena had looked up in surprise to find Mr. Karpels grinning at her.

"My Johnny Apple doesn't give such presents to just anyone," he had said. "You must be someone quite special."

"What a clever horse he is," Lena said admiringly.

"Ah, but more than just clever," Mr. Karpels had replied solemnly. He then told Lena how, on the previous day, they had been selling fruit outside the yeshiva on 14th Street. Some of the young scholars were arguing over the Talmud, and one of them had quoted a passage incorrectly. He had paid no attention to Johnny Apple's indignant snorts, and not until an overripe peach knocked his yarmulke off did he realize his error.

This story thrilled Lena. "If a horse can know the Talmud," she had thought, "surely so can I!" Lena had a thousand questions to ask about this wondrous horse. Where did he come from? How had he learned the Talmud? What other things did he know? But before Lena could open her mouth, Mr. Karpels and Johnny Apple did something which left even Lena speechless.

With a twinkle in his eye, Mr. Karpels had tossed fruit in the air, pears, apples, even a cluster of grapes, and deftly Johnny returned them with a toss of his muzzle. Lena watched spellbound as horse and fruit seller kept the fruit aloft with their juggling for several minutes, by which time it was bruised and unsaleable. "You see," Karpels had concluded, "Johnny Apple's teacher was not only a learned rabbi, but also an accomplished juggler. Johnny Apple himself is as skilled as any of the great rabbinical jugglers about whom the Talmud teaches us. Once he even kept aloft eight flaming torches, a feat not seen since the great Rabbi Shimon ben Gamaliel! In the old country he was called Herschel the Wonder Horse, and I was Karpelashovsky the Juggler, but here"—Karpels shrugged philosophically—"here we have American names, and we sell apples. So it goes, so it goes."

To Lena's delight and amazement, Mr. Karpels had answered all her unspoken questions. But then a new question had occurred to Lena. Breathlessly, she asked, "Mr. Karpels, I have always wanted to study the Talmud, but I have had no one to guide me in this study. Could he . . . would you . . . do you think that Johnny Apple could teach me the Talmud?"

"I think we should let Johnny answer that question, don't you?" Mr. Karpels had replied with a smile.

Johnny whinnied and nodded enthusiastically. Mr. Karpels had found some old Hebrew books for Lena, and from that moment on, Lena spent every spare moment with Johnny Apple. It was slow going—Johnny could correct her only with snorts and whinnies—but Lena had made a beginning. She hoped to work on a particularly difficult tractate of the Mishnah today.

As Lena approached the corner of Hester and Orchard, she noticed that a crowd had gathered and she heard shouting. Another anarchist, Lena thought, making speeches. But then she began to distinguish words— "What is this you do? Have you stolen another apple from me? Do you take me for a fool?" Frantically Lena pushed her way through the tightly packed crowd. Breaking through the front ranks, she saw Johnny Apple, but the man beside him was not kindly old Mr. Karpels, but a much younger man with a scowl on his face. The man brandished a horse whip at Johnny Apple, shouting, "You useless horse, I'll teach you to steal from me!"

Lena stood, frozen with horror. But before the lash could fall, a girl about Lena's age—at least Lena thought it was a girl, for she was so ragged and dirty it was difficult to tell—threw herself in front of Johnny Apple. Her voice, when she spoke, was unexpectedly sweet, like a bird in Corlears Park. "I'm sorry, mister! Johnny always gives me an apple for a present. I . . . he . . . we did not mean to do anything wrong!" The man's face grew redder and redder as he stood there, still holding the whip over his head. Then cries began to rise up from the gathered crowd.

"What are you going to do? Beat the girl?"

"Leave the beast alone, man!"

"Can't you see that the horse was only doing a *mitzvah?*"

Finally, the man threw the whip back into the cart and, without a word, sullenly led the unfortunate animal away. Lena realized, with a sinking feeling, there would be no Hebrew lesson today. What had happened to Mr. Karpels? Who was this new man? And most importantly, who was this other girl, to whom Johnny Apple also gave presents?

Lena turned back along Hester Street, her quick eyes looking everywhere for the ragged girl. But though she searched from Orchard to Essex, the girl seemed to have vanished without a trace. As Lena reluctantly turned homeward, she saw a skirt peddler jostle the chickpea cart, upsetting several paper cones of the steaming, savory chickpeas. As the two men argued loudly in Yiddish, the ragged girl appeared out of nowhere, and began crawling on the ground like a dog, feverishly gathering up the dirty chickpeas.

"You, girl—" Lena began, but the ragged girl only looked at her fearfully, before darting around the corner. Lena raced after the girl, and found her crouched behind a pile of trash, devouring the chickpeas, heedless of their coating of dirt. Lena opened her mouth to speak, but when she looked into the girl's bright blue eyes, Lena felt a jolt as if she had touched the wires along which the trolley cars ran, and all her many questions flew out of her head. The ragged girl clutched the chickpeas fearfully. To set her at ease, Lena quickly said, "Do not be afraid. I am a friend of Johnny Apple. Are you his friend as well?"

The girl replied with enthusiasm, "Oh yes! He is such a clever horse. When I talk to him, I know that he understands just what I am saying. And oh, he does such wonderful tricks." As the girl spoke, Lena noticed how thin her face was and how her beautiful blue eyes burned feverishly in their deep sockets, and also how a strong stench rose up from her, like the East River on a hot summer day.

"Where do you come from? Why do you live like this?" Lena questioned her.

The girl hesitated a moment before she spoke. " I am an orphan and have nothing but the streets to call my home. I come from Russia. My mother died three years ago and my father said that we should travel to the new world and make a new start. But he died soon after we landed, and he has made his new start in heaven with my mother."

"I am so sorry for your misfortunes," Lena said, tears springing to her eyes. "I, too, am from Russia. My parents came here eight years ago, when I was seven. What is your name?"

"I am called Lily."

"And I am Lena." Lena had a thousand questions she wanted to ask the other girl. Where did she sleep? How would she survive the coming winter? Did she realize how badly she smelled? But the sun was setting and she must go home. "Lily, meet me here tomorrow, so we may talk some more. Since we are both friends of Johnny Apple, we must be friends as well, *nu?*"

Lily smiled for the first time. "Yes, yes! I would like another friend."

"*Shabbat shalom,* Lily," Lena called over her shoulder as she hurried away.

"*Shabbat shalom?*" Lily repeated in puzzlement.

Lena ran the ten blocks home, but when she reached the rickety steps of her family's tenement, she slowed her pace. She'd be in trouble—again. If only there was a way to creep in without anyone noticing. But in their two-room apartment, with one room rented out to boarders, there was no place to hide. Why couldn't she be more like Moishe or Golda? Lena's older brother spent all his time on his studies, and never gave his parents a moment's worry. Golda was a beautiful baby, playing contentedly for hours with a bar of soap while Mama bent over the washtub. Only Lena was a problem.

Lena opened the door and slipped in as quietly as possible, but it was no use. The family was seated around the table that was always moved into the center of the room on *shabbes*, and Mama was ladling out the soup. Everyone looked up.

"Lena, *vee bis du gevoren*?" Each word came out with a jerk, as Lena's mother angrily splashed soup into bowls.

Even though she was in trouble, Lena could not repress her irritation at her mother's old-world ways. "In English, Mama, in English. We are in America now," Lena reminded her mother as she slipped into her place.

"Yes, my daughter, you are right. Ve are in America now, vere ze children run vild. So I ask you in English. Vere haf you been? And vere are de pickles?" At the last of the carefully enunciated English words, Mama set the tureen down with a thump, splashing Lena with scalding soup.

The pickles! Lena had forgotten them completely. Shamefaced, she laid the pennies on the table. "I stopped for just a moment to visit with Johnny Apple," she tried to explain, "and there was a big crowd and the fruit man was going to beat him and—"

"Johnny Apple?" Mama said as she threw up her hands. "Again vith the horse! Vat about your father and your brother Moishe? Is this how it is done in America, that young girls vorry about horses, vile ze men go hungry?"

"And you were almost out after sunset," reproved Moishe. "You are being infected by *goyische* ways."

"Did ve raise you to turn your back on your faith?" asked Papa sadly.

"But that I would never do. Papa, I wish only to honor my faith by studying the Talmud," Lena replied.

"Enough." Her father held up his hand. "The Talmud teaches us: *Me shemelamed bito Tora, ke ilu melamed teeflut*. That is all you need to know."

"But Papa—" Lena began, frustrated as usual when Papa argued in the language she was forbidden to study.

"It is not for a child to qvestion the visdom of a parent. Do you vish to end up like Shmuel?" Lena's father ended the familiar discussion as he often did.

"But what *did* become of Uncle Shmuel?" Lena asked curiously, as she always did when Shmuel was mentioned.

"That name is not to be spoken in my home!" her father said with finality. He continued in an exasperated tone, "Enough vith your qvestions, daughter—let us eat now."

Although she hadn't seen him since she was a little girl in Russia, many of Lena's fondest memories were of her beloved Uncle Shmuel, who had always been ready with a joke or a trick. He was like Johnny Apple that way. Then

Uncle Shmuel had disappeared and Lena's grandfather had declared that he had only one son, even going so far as to sit *shiva* for Shmuel. Since that day, all of Lena's questions about Shmuel had been met with scolding.

But now, as Lena sipped her hot soup, searching hopefully for a morsel of meat that might not have ended up in her father's or Moishe's bowl, her thoughts were busy with Lily. Poor Lily had none of Mama's good, hot soup, only some trampled chickpeas to still her hunger. "Tomorrow I will bring her a bone," Lena decided, "so that she might have a little marrow to keep up her strength." Caught up in her own thoughts, Lena did not notice the melancholy air that hung over the dinner table until the fresh challah bread was passed. Looking around for an explanation, she noticed something else.

"Where are Mr. Malkovitch and Mr. Kalman?" she asked. Immediately her Mama threw her apron over her head and began to wail loudly, while her father raged, "Those thieving boarders! Two weeks rent they owe, and they steal away, taking our featherbed!" His shoulders slumped down, and he raised his eyes to the ceiling. "Oh, Master of the Universe, why were we chosen to suffer so?"

Moishe offered tentatively, "Perhaps, Papa, you could get me a job at the facto—"

Papa's eyes flew down, and Mama uncovered her head. "No!" they chorused. Moishe looked relieved. "You vill be a scholar, my son," Papa added. "But you, my daughter," he said, turning to Lena, "ve have plans for you. You vill be an obedient daughter, *nu?*"

"Yes," chimed in Mama, "there vill be no more running after horses."

Lena sat still, thinking hard. Her parents must be planning to take her out of school to work in one of the factories sewing, like her cousin Minnie, who worked at the Triangle Shirtwaist Factory. Suddenly she had a brilliant idea—if Lily could get a job there as well, she could be the family's new boarder! She lifted her head and smiled at her parents. "Yes, I will help."

Lena awoke that Saturday, filled with anticipation. She did not mind as much that left-out feeling she always had when Moishe and her father left for the synagogue. She waited until Mama had also left, carrying Golda, to visit Tante Rivka. Then Lena carefully wrapped a bone up in a rag and tucked it, along with a bar of her mother's laundry soap, under her shawl.

Lily was sitting glumly in the doorway of a shuttered shop. When Lena appeared, Lily jumped to her feet and smiled. "I knew you'd come!"

Lena quickly pulled the rag out from beneath her shawl. "Look what I brought you!" she announced, her brown eyes dancing with delight.

Lily unwrapped the napkin and gasped. "What a lovely bone! I have not had such a treat since I left my homeland!" With her strong white teeth, she cracked the bone, and in an instant she had sucked out all the marrow and licked the rag for any traces of grease it might hold.

"And look what else," Lena said with excitement as she pulled out the bar of laundry soap.

"For me!" Lily gasped again as she licked her greasy fingers. Then she looked around in bewilderment. "But where will I wash?"

"You must wash in the East River," Lena decreed. "It is still September." Lily looked somewhat daunted, but obedient to her new friend's commands, she followed her to a secluded part of the embankment, where she shed her fetid rags and gingerly climbed into the chilly gray river.

"The river is as dirty as me," she said through chattering teeth. "Are you sure it will make me clean?"

"Yes, because you will scrub yourself all over with this," said Lena firmly, handing her the laundry soap. While Lily scrubbed her body and clothes, Lena told Lily excitedly of her plan—how they would both get jobs in the Triangle Shirtwaist Factory, and how Lily would board with Lena's family. Lily's eyes were already full of tears from the cold water and harsh soap, but now they overflowed with tears of joy. "The Virgin Mary has at last answered my prayers!" she cried. "I will light a candle before her icon at St. Gregory's as soon as I get my first week's wages!"

Lena felt almost dizzy with disbelief. Her head all awhirl; she tried to make sense of this shocking news. "But . . . you said you came from Russia."

"Yes," said Lily, somewhat bewildered. "I was born in Novgorod, but we lived in a small village in the steppes, where my father was stationed with the Tsar's army."

"A cossack!" Lena started back in horror. Her family had fled Russia because of the cossacks and their terrible pogroms. Lena would have run away if Lily, belatedly realizing the meaning of Lena's distress, had not grasped at her arm with damp fingers, almost pulling her into the river. "Wait! It is true I am a cossack's daughter and my parents taught me to despise the godless Jews. But here in America I have learned that there are as many kind Jews as vile ones. And it is true the priests taught us that all the Jews would one day burn in hell, but I am sure that for a Jewess as beautiful as you, there must be a place in heaven." Her blue eyes looked at Lena beseechingly.

Lena thought hard. "It is true that your people have persecuted the Jews since before the time of my ancestors'

ancestors, but at the settlement house Miss Taylor has been kinder to me than my own mother, and my cousin Minnie numbers many *goyim* among her friends."

As she looked at the shivering Christian girl, Lena felt the prejudices of the Old World falling away, and it was like setting down a heavy basket of laundry. She embraced Lily, ignoring the cold, soapy water, and Lily returned the embrace with fervor. Suddenly Lena became conscious that she was standing in the East River with her arms around a naked girl. "You must get dressed now," she said, blushing, "or you will catch cold. Then we will go find Johnny Apple and tell him we are friends."

Now that Lily had washed, her skin gleamed milky white, and her hair shone pale yellow, like the straw that lined Johnny Apple's stall. The two girls walked hand in hand to the livery stable, stealing shy glances at each other.

"Do I still smell?" asked the Christian girl fearfully.

"Only of carbolic soap," Lena reassured her. Then, "Oof!" said Lena. She had tripped over the old Pretzel Woman again! Only the Pretzel Woman would be out on the street when all the other peddlers and pushcart owners were observing the Sabbath. "Excuse my carelessness, Pretzel Woman," Lena apologized.

The Pretzel Woman only hummed a Yiddish tune, as if she had not felt the blow. Perhaps she hadn't, thought Lena, she was so well padded. Then the old woman cast a shrewd glance at the two girls and croaked, "This is your sister, *nu?*"

Lena wondered if the old woman was slightly crazy. No one would mistake her and Lily for sisters. "No, Pretzel Woman, we have not the same parents." Then Lena thought for a moment and added, "But I love Lily as if she were a kind of sister."

"And I feel the same way about Lena," Lily said shyly.

The old woman fixed her eyes on the girls with an unblinking stare. "So, you are not sisters, yet you feel like sisters. Yes. I see it. And that, too, is a kind of sisterhood. A very powerful sisterhood." She paused, swaying back and forth a little. "But this power is best kept hidden."

"Yes, Pretzel Woman," the girls chorused obediently. As soon as they were out of her sight, they looked at each other puzzled.

"The Pretzel Woman often speaks strangely," said Lily.

"Yes," Lena admitted, "usually I can understand her meaning, but this time I cannot."

Lily knew where to find Johnny Apple, in a dilapidated old stable on Willett Street. No one was there to prevent the girls from creeping in to visit their friend. The horse was asleep on his feet and Lena was shocked at how gaunt Johnny looked. "Oh Lily, is he sick?" she whispered. "What happened to Mr. Karpels, who used to care for him so tenderly?"

"I don't know," worried Lily. "For a week I saw not hide nor hair of Mr. Karpels or Johnny Apple. Then yesterday this new man appeared. Perhaps," she added hopefully, "Mr. Karpels has run off to join the circus, for you know he worked in the carnival as a youth."

Lily tried to imagine Mr. Karpels in a circus, but she had a foreboding that this happy fate was not his. "He would never leave Johnny Apple to be mistreated," she said. "Look at this old hay! Mr. Karpels would give him oats and bran mashes!"

"When we work at the factory, we will buy him oats and the other things he needs," exclaimed Lily, who looked forward to working in the sweatshop as the solution to all their problems.

Their conversation had woken the horse, who nickered his welcome to the two girls. "See, Johnny Apple, we are friends now," said Lena. The horse whinnied approval.

"Like two sisters," added Lily, putting her arm around Lena. Again Lena felt that electric jolt. Was this the power the Pretzel Woman had meant, this electricity that lit her up inside?

Johnny Apple snorted indignantly. The girls looked at each other puzzled, and then Lena understood.

"Like two sisters *and a brother*, is that better, Johnny?"

Johnny Apple shook his head up and down and neighed enthusiastically. Unable to contain himself, he balanced the laundry soap, the remains of the bone, and a clump of hay in a tower on his nose. As she and Lily applauded the horse's trick, Lena realized that, although neither Lily nor Johnny were of The Chosen People, they were for her a kind of family—a chosen family.

When she hurried home that afternoon, leaving Johnny Apple chewing his old hay, and Lily curled up in the stairwell of a condemned building, Lena was full of happy plans. Of course, she would not tell her family about Lily just yet. Lily needed to look more presentable before Lena could introduce her as a prospective boarder. And she wasn't sure how the family would react to her friendship with a *schiksa*. Monday she'd see Minnie about getting those jobs at the Triangle Shirtwaist Factory. Lena realized she had a busy week ahead.

But on Monday, Lena despaired at first of escaping the tenement apartment, for Mama told her she would no longer go to school. There were no laundry deliveries to make, but piles of dirty linens to wash. Lena and Mama labored over tubs of wet sheets, until suddenly Mama exclaimed:

"*Oy vey,* woe is me! The laundry soap, it is gone already. Here, Lena, take a penny and buy a new bar."

Lena danced away, and once the laundry soap was purchased and tucked under her arm, she hurried to the Shirtwaist Factory. Fortune was indeed smiling on her today, for Minnie was outside, eating her lunch with a crowd of cheerful girls. Lena quickly explained her plan and Minnie smiled.

"You're in luck! Frieda Friedman has consumption and Gussie Shashefsky cut her finger off with a pair of pinking shears! I will tell the boss this afternoon, and he will keep those places for you."

A whistle blew. "Come, girls, back to work," called Minnie, smiling. "Our ten minutes are up." Lena's eyes widened enviously as the girls wrapped up their lunch things and shook out their skirts in a leisurely fashion. A whole ten minutes, just to eat! The future looked rosy indeed. Lena didn't even mind the scolding Mama gave her for being so slow fetching the soap.

That night, Lena bubbled over with excitement when she saw Lily waiting at the cozy spot beneath the Williamsburg Bridge where they had arranged to meet. Lena breathlessly shared her news about the jobs that now awaited them.

"Oh, Lena," Lily said rapturously, "now we will be together all the time and we shall have money to buy good food for our Johnny Apple. Is there no end to the happiness you bring me?"

She pulled Lena to her in a joyful embrace, and in so doing, her lips brushed against Lena's. Again Lena felt an electric jolt, this time stronger than ever. If this was what it felt like to grab hold of the trolley car wires, Lena wondered, what would it feel like to follow those wires all the way to the end of the line? *This* was a question to which she *must* find the answer. Shyly, she leaned toward Lily until their lips met again, and Lena did not pull away until the trolley had circled the city many times. Then she paused only long enough to declare joyfully, "Now I know that it is you, darling Lily, who is my *beshert*, the one who is meant for me."

Lena redoubled her efforts over the next few days as she prepared for her life with Lily. She begged a worn-out dress for Lily from Minnie, promising to pay her for it as soon as she was earning wages. She stole food from the family's table for Lily. She worked into the night ironing mounds of laundry, hoping to win her mama's and papa's approval with her diligence and obedience. For her part, Lily sorted through the trash from the gutter, selling bits of metal and rags to the rag collectors for pennies, which she used to buy small bags of oats for Johnny Apple, ignoring her own ravenous hunger.

On Saturday, Lena decided, she would tell her parents of her plan. They had seemed more cheerful of late, and would perhaps be receptive. She had told Lily to come before the noon meal, so that she could introduce her as a prospective boarder. If all went well, her parents might even invite Lily to share their meal, and for once Lily would have hot food in her belly.

"Mama, Papa, I have been thinking how I may help our family," she began as Mama slid a kugel into the oven while Papa pored over the Midrash.

"Yes, my darling, ve too haf been thinking." Mama nodded with a pleased expression. "Your Papa and me, ve came to America so that you may haf a better life. Ve do not want that you should work in the factories. Your Papa and me, ve do not mind that our fingers haf become gnarled and our backs hunched. Ve do not mind that our health is broken though ve are not yet forty years of age, but for you, ve vant better."

"But Mama, I would not mind to work in the factories. I have found a place in the Triangle Shirtwaist Factory, where Minnie works."

To Lena's dismay, neither Papa nor Mama seemed particularly pleased with her idea.

"You think ve vant that you should become like that Minnie who defies her parents and spends her vages on clothing and the nickelodeon, and says she vill find her own husband?" Papa said reprovingly, closing his book.

"But Papa—" Lena began.

"No, my little Lena, ve haf another plan," Papa said, barely able to contain his glee.

There was a knock at the door. Lily, already! Lena dashed to open it. She could only hope this part of her plan would work better.

But it was not Lily at the door. Instead, there stood the cruel fruit seller, who had so mysteriously replaced Mr. Karpels! In a daze, Lena stood aside to let him enter, as Papa beamed and said, "Welcome to our home. It is a great happiness upon us that you should join us for our humble meal."

The fruit seller looked Lena over, like a dairy farmer inspecting a cow, as Papa continued, "Yosef Karpels, may I present to you my daughter, Lena, your future bride, if you vill thus honor our family."

Lena stood in stunned silence, until Moishe prompted her, "Thank our parents for their goodness, my sister."

Lena began to respond automatically, "Thank you, Pa—" before her brain started working again. "But you are not

Mr. Karpels! What has happened to Mr. Karpels? Why do you now drive his fruit cart?"

Lena's parents looked down in shame as the man laughed and said in a jovial tone, "She is very beautiful, as I was promised, but I was not told that she was such a curious girl."

"Lena," Mama said sharply, "is this how you treat the man you are to marry?"

"I do not mind. I like a girl with spirit," interjected the new Karpels, fingering the whip he always carried. Then he turned to Lena. "In answer to your questions, my uncle, Isaac Karpels, passed away two weeks ago, and now I, Yosef Karpels, own the fruit cart, along with that good-for-nothing horse, Johnny Apple."

Lena quickly leapt to the defense of her friend. "Johnny Apple is not good-for-nothing! He is the smartest horse in the whole world!"

"My uncle was a sentimental old man," Karpels replied contemptuously. "That horse destroys more fruit with his foolish tricks than I sell. But I have a strong back and I have gotten myself a pushcart. I will save money on horse feed and I will gain fifteen dollars when I sell the useless beast to the glue factory!"

Lena stood frozen in horror as her father praised, "A smart businessman, *nu?*"

Just then a timid voice spoke from the doorway. "I have come about a room to be rented?" It was Lily. To Lena, she looked like an angel from paradise in her patched gown, but the three adults stared at her in bewilderment. Karpels spoke first, recognition dawning in his eyes. "You are the ragged girl from the streets, who I have seen sneaking around my horse and stealing my apples! What nonsense is this about renting a room? Be off with you, little thief!"

Lena leaped to Lily's side. "This is Lily, the girl I love. Insult her at your peril!" she cried.

Now Karpels shook with anger. "I pity the poor fellow who marries this *meshugeh* girl!" he shouted as he slammed out of the tiny apartment.

Papa raised his arms up and looked toward the heavens in silent reproach, while Mama wailed, "Oh, Merciful One, what have we done to deserve such a wicked daughter?"

Bewildered and frightened by this unexpected turn of events, Lily crossed herself and murmured a rapid prayer in Russian.

Papa's eyes bulged. "This girl is a Christian!" he gasped.

"And a Russian!" Mama shrieked.

"Haf you forgotten, Lena, vat those villainous cossacks did to our people?" Lena's shocked father demanded.

"My father was stationed on the steppes, far from the Jews," Lily protested.

"Oh, Creator of the Universe, vat haf I done that mine own flesh and blood should bring a cossack's daughter into our home?" cried Mama.

Now Papa turned to Lily and began, "I vish upon you that you should find yourself living in a mansion with a thousand rooms, and in each room a thousand beds . . ."

Lily smiled at this unexpected friendliness.

". . . and may you be found dead in every one of those beds, you cossack's daughter!"

Lily reeled at the cruel, yet clever, conclusion to the curse, while Lena leapt to her defense. "This is America, we are not in Russia any longer," cried Lena. "There are no cossacks in America. Here it does not matter who is

Jew and who is Christian! What is important is that Lily is my friend, and we are all Americans!"

Lena's father shook his finger angrily. "Alvays vith these new ideas! So is my daughter now a freethinker? Do you vish to end up like Shmuel?"

Again with Shmuel, Lena thought. Her father continued ranting.

"The great Rabbi Gamaliel said, 'Do His will as if it were thy will, that He may do thy will as if it were His will.' It is not for a girl to defy this visdom. You try to set the vorld upon its head, acting as if horses and women are equal vith men."

Horses! Suddenly Lena remembered Johnny Apple and his impending fate—there was no time now for a Talmudic debate! She raced out the door, dragging the frightened Lily behind her. "Come! We must save Johnny Apple!"

It was not difficult for Lily to distract the stable boy while Lena led Johnny Apple out of his stall, but once the trio was on the street, they did not know what to do next. They had no one to turn to, and soon the police would be after the two girls for theft. They must leave the Lower East Side, but to go where? Where could a clever horse who knew some tricks, a disobedient Jewish girl who only wished to study the Talmud, and an orphaned Christian girl who was always hungry find their place in the world?

"Ooof!" Once again, Lena had tripped over the Pretzel Woman. "Does she never go home?" Lena wondered. "Again, I ask your pardon, Pretzel Woman," she said politely.

The Pretzel Woman's bright eyes, buried deep in her wrinkled face, took in Lily's tears, Lena's defiant air, and the presence of Johnny Apple. She hummed a little Yiddish tune, swaying back and forth, while Johnny tapped his hoof in time. "So!" she said at last. "You did not listen to the Pretzel Woman. You did not keep hidden what should be kept hidden. And so evil has befallen you."

The girls hung their heads. Lena wondered if perhaps the wisdom of the old Pretzel Woman could help them with their current difficulties. "O Pretzel Woman," said Lena, "we are three friends who wish only to stay together, though the world tries to drive us apart. Do you have any advice for us?"

The Pretzel Woman's voice took on a tender, crooning tone. "Is it wisdom the girl wants, or information? Wisdom I give you freely, with maybe a stale, two-day-old pretzel." She pulled a pretzel out from the depths of her shawl, and Lily pounced on it with her usual appetite. "Johnny Apple is a horse with some talents and you girls are a mismatched set that fits together. You must find a place where the strange is ordinary and the ordinary strange."

Lena and Lily stared blankly at each other, then back at the Pretzel Woman, who spoke again, "Wisdom I give freely, but information will cost you three cents."

The girls pooled their pennies, and were able to meet the Pretzel Woman's price with a penny to spare. When the money was safely in her hand, the old woman cackled and coughed for some minutes before uttering two words, "Coney Island."

Coney Island! The two girls stared at each other, as understanding dawned. They had heard of this fabled land of amusements and delights across the waters. Minnie had gone with her factory friends, and Miss Taylor had promised to take the settlement children one day, but neither Lily nor Lena had ever been.

"How will we get there?" queried Lily worriedly. But the Pretzel Woman seemed to have gone to sleep.

Lena thought hard. Minnie had taken a ferry, and Miss Taylor had promised they would ride on the cars, but neither of these would be possible with Johnny Apple.

"We must walk," she said firmly.

And so began their weary trudge, downtown to the Brooklyn Bridge, then across the bridge and into Brooklyn, always keeping close to the water, for they knew Coney Island was on the shore. Lena led the trio and Lily cheered all their spirits by talking about the good things they would eat in Coney Island. Johnny Apple helped as well, kicking the sailors who stumbled out of waterfront taverns and tried to pinch the girls, and nipping at the boys who jeered, "Whyncha riding yer old nag?" Though it might have eased their own journey, neither girl could bear to ride their weary friend. Soon there were no more houses and they passed only warehouses, and the occasional soap factory. As night fell, these too disappeared, and the road was bordered only by empty fields.

They had fallen silent, each secretly thinking they were hopelessly lost, when Johnny whinnied urgently. The two girls looked up, and saw a distant glow in the sky. Johnny broke into a shambling trot, and the girls ran after him. Soon the glow became the electric lights of an amusement park, and the sounds of music and laughter reached the girls' ears. Looking up, they saw cars racing down the steep slopes of a roller coaster, and heard the delighted screams of the passengers. They passed dance halls and beer gardens, and saw signs promising even more wondrous sights—a village populated entirely by midgets, a girl with a thousand eyes, incubators holding tiny premature babies! Lily's eyes were like saucers as she looked around at the vendors selling chowder, fried clams, and a special sausage on a bun called a red hot. They drifted along with the happy crowds until they came upon beautiful white buildings with towers and minarets outlined in a thousand electric lights, which spelled out the word "Dreamland."

"We made it, we made it!" they cried, realizing finally that their ordeal was over. The two girls joyfully embraced while Johnny Apple capered about like a colt. The three friends were about to enter Dreamland, but stopped abruptly at a sign that said "Admission 25 cents." Even in this wonderland, Lena realized, her heart sinking, cold hard cash was still necessary. She wondered if there were shirtwaist factories, or laundries where she and Lily could find work.

"Never mind, Lena," Lily said gently. "I know we will go to Dreamland, someday."

Lena knew that if Lily, who hadn't had a solid meal in months, could bear up under the disappointment, she could too. "Well, we still have a penny," she said. "Here! Why don't you buy yourself one of those red hots?"

"Oh Lena, I could not spend our last penny," Lily replied.

Lena surveyed her beloved and said candidly, "My beautiful Lily, you are as thin as a dried-up herring. Nothing could please me more than to see you grow as plump and round as a delicious piece of gefilte fish. Now go, buy the red hot."

Lena's talk of food had left Lily unable to resist any longer. She darted away to the nearest stand, and while she paid for her purchase, Lena and Johnny idly watched a nearby sideshow.

"See Sammy the Sword Swallower, who has entertained the crowned heads of Europe. Watch him swallow rapiers, knives, and sabres of all description . . ." The man's patter went on, and he held back the tent flap to display the sword swallower, a tall handsome man in an embroidered cape, holding up a small sword. Then—

"Uncle Shmuel!" Lena screamed.

The sword swallower started in surprise, and tossing his sword aside, he leaped off the stage and gathered his niece in a warm embrace. Johnny Apple caught the sword and balanced it on his nose, as the crowd applauded both the heartwarming reunion and the talented horse.

"Can this be my little Lena?" cried Uncle Shmuel, gazing at his niece.

"This . . . this has been your fate?" Lena exclaimed wonderingly, looking around the gay boardwalk. She had pictured something much worse. Lena bubbled over with questions. "Why did you leave our family? How did you come to be here?"

"Ah, my Lenalinke, still with a thousand questions." Uncle Shmuel laughed gaily. "How sad I was to leave you, but my father could not understand that I did not wish to be a rabbi, I wished only to entertain the common people." A distant sadness passed like a cloud through Uncle Shmuel's eyes. "When he found out that I had apprenticed myself to a sword swallower, he cast me out of my home, and cautioned me never to return."

"My troubles, Uncle, are perhaps not so different from yours," Lena explained. "My father could never understand that all I wanted was to study the Talmud, and be with my friends Johnny Apple and Lily."

"And is this your Lily?" Uncle Shmuel asked.

Lily was standing a few feet away, politely letting the uncle and niece become reacquainted, while she gulped down her red hot.

"Yes," Lena said proudly, "this is my Lily."

"Ahhh, what a *shayna maidel.* You have chosen well, my niece," said Uncle Shmuel as he looked kindly at the pretty blond girl.

"Ang oo," said Lily, her mouth still full of the red hot.

"And this is Johnny Apple." Lena pointed to the horse, still balancing the sword. Again Uncle Shmuel started in surprise.

"Why, this is Herschel the Wonder Horse!" he cried. "The most talented horse in the world! We were on the same bill in Odessa. How often I have wondered what became of him!"

"He is ours now," said Lena, "but I do not know how I will provide the oats he needs, or these red hots for Lily." She looked worriedly at Lily, who was licking her fingers.

Uncle Shmuel clapped his hands decisively. "Worry no longer, little one! Herschel—that is, Johnny Apple—will have a part in my act! Why, with his talents, I can double my money! And perhaps this little maid might sell these red hots, of which she is clearly so fond."

"God bless America!" cried a rapturous Lily.

Uncle Shmuel then turned to Lena. "And you, my dear, you shall study the Talmud and earn money too! Here in Coney Island, the visitors like to look at the babies in their incubators. Why should they not also pay to see a young girl studying the Talmud?"

Lena grew concerned. "But would it not be wrong to use the Talmud in this way for earthly gain?" She was surprised when the response to her question came not from Shmuel or Johnny, but from Lily.

"But did not the great Rabbi Gamaliel say, 'Comely is study of Torah with worldly occupation, for toil in both makes sins forgotten'?"

Shmuel and Lena stared in amazement at the blond girl, who offered, "Johnny Apple has been teaching me as well."

"So he has." Uncle Shmuel laughed. "So he has. But enough talk of work—for your first night in Coney Island, we must celebrate!" And so saying, he paid the four entrance fees and led the three friends through the gates of Dreamland.

Lady Snow

Julie Creighton stood in the corner of the sunken living room, holding her Shirley Temple and looking out the window as if she were fascinated by the view of Palm Beach. In reality it was too dark to see anything more than her own reflection—an average-looking girl with brown feathered hair and anxious eyes.

Nervously she smoothed her new Jordache blue jeans, hoping no one would guess how out of place she felt. They'd looked great in the motel room, but she stood out like a sore thumb in the snowstorm of white Guess jeans everyone else was wearing. She just didn't belong in this fancy, ocean-front condo. She didn't belong at this party. Why had she come?

Julie bit her lip and her reflection did too. They both knew why she'd come—she'd come for Brittany.

Brittany was the top rider on the show jumping circuit and had been for years. Sure, there'd been rivals from time to time, riders that looked as if they might unseat Brittany from her throne, but they never seemed to have her staying power. They might start strong, but by the end of the season they always fell apart, making stupid mistakes while Brittany maintained her calm perfection. Pressure never bothered Brittany. She was the girl who had everything—wealth, talent, beauty—and winning was in her blood.

This was Brittany's party, to celebrate the opening of the Citrus Classic, the final show of the Florida circuit. Julie had never ridden the winter circuit before, having only graduated from high school the previous June, but even so she'd heard about the notoriously lavish parties that Brittany threw at her cousin Blaine's condo, where she stayed every winter.

Julie glanced covertly around the room. No Brittany so far, but everyone else who was anyone in show jumping was there. Owners, trainers, riders, and even track officials mingled on the deep-pile carpet. There were the de Cuysters and their new trainer Lance; there was Jillian, who used to ride for that Virginia couple, but now rode for the Lilienthalers. And there was Ashley Morgan at the bar, talking to a trainer and looking like a pale imitation of Brittany.

Last season Ashley and Brittany had been inseparable. It had been Ashley and Brittany having drinks at the Hunt Club, Ashley and Brittany arriving at the shows in Brittany's Porsche, Ashley and Brittany sharing a condo in New York. The word had been that it was going to be a breakout year for Ashley and her horse, Stardust. But though they'd started the season with a string of victories, by the time the Grand Prix rolled around, Ashley appeared pallid and jumpy and Stardust looked even worse. They hadn't even placed.

Julie turned to peer at the group of people by the fireplace. No Brittany there either, but wait—was that Caro

Carmichael, sitting and staring at the flames? Yes, it must be her, because there was a set of crutches leaning against her chair. Two years ago she'd seemed a sure thing to beat Brittany—until that terrible accident. Julie shivered a little, remembering, and turned back to the window.

Now there was serious talk that Julie might be the one to end Brittany's Grand Prix winning streak—her, Julie Creighton! She stared at her reflection. Was this really the girl who would beat Brittany Fairchild? This ordinary girl with average looks and no money, just an honest determination to do the best with what she had? And what she had was her horse, Lady Snow. Julie smiled just thinking of her. And then there were the years of training she'd gotten from Liz Halstead—one of the best riders around and Julie's best friend. That is, Liz *had* been her best friend—before The Incident.

Julie shuddered. Her reflection shuddered too. Neither of them wanted to think about that again. Instead, she thought about Brittany. The way she'd suddenly appeared at the stall door that afternoon, while Julie was grooming Lady Snow. Julie had never been so close to Brittany before, close enough to see how blue her eyes were and how even her tan was, close enough to smell the mixture of hay and Opium that clung to her. Julie had stood there, staring at her idol in wonderment.

And Brittany had smiled, a dazzling, perfect smile. "Julie. Party at Blaine's tonight. Be there." That was all Brittany said. That was all she needed to say.

Suddenly, cries of "Hi, Brittany!" "Brittany, hey, where have you been?" brought Julie back to the present. She turned around. Her reflection turned around too, but she wasn't watching it anymore. Because Brittany was standing in the doorway, surveying the party with a small smile on her lips. The lights picked up the gold in her hair, which fell in smooth waves on her cream-colored cashmere cowl-neck sweater. She wasn't wearing Guess jeans. Instead she wore wide-wale cords in a vivid shade of pink. In a week, everyone else would be wearing them too.

Her eyes met Julie's, and she came straight to her, ignoring the partiers who tried to catch her attention. Without asking permission, she picked up Julie's drink and took a sip. That was Brittany. Taking what she wanted. And no one ever minded, because she was Brittany. Her eyes sparkled at Julie over the rim of the glass. "Where'd you get this, the kiddie table?" She laughed, a silvery laugh. "Let's get you a real drink."

Julie followed Brittany toward the teak wet bar in the corner, a little uncertain. The truth was, she hadn't ever *had* a real drink. And she was thinking about what Liz had said to her, the morning she'd left for Florida. She'd been loading Lady Snow into the trailer when Liz had appeared. They'd been avoiding each other for weeks, and Julie's heart had jumped with hope when she saw Liz walking toward her. But Liz had only come to deliver a brusque warning: "Stay away from alcohol and drugs and from . . . from the people who use them. They can make you do things—things you thought you would never do."

Brittany looked up from the drink she was mixing, and smiled. "I'm going to make you my favorite drink, okay?"

"Okay," said Julie. Liz's warning seemed silly. How could a drink make her do something she didn't want to? And it had hurt—the *only* time Liz had spoken to her since The Incident and it was just to give her the same old sermon Julie had been hearing since sixth grade! Well, Julie decided, she was sick of Liz and all her preaching—after all, Julie was eighteen now, an adult, whether Liz realized it or not!

Brittany handed Julie a glass filled with a clear liquid, a little sliver of lime perched precariously on its edge. Julie sipped tentatively. She had tried beer once and hadn't liked it. But this—this didn't taste too bad at all. She took a bigger sip, smiling at Brittany. Brittany laughed her silvery laugh again. "Looks like gin and tonic is your drink!" she said with pleasure. She raised her glass. "Here's to those blue ribbons you've been winning!"

Julie felt a warm glow spread through her. Brittany was so nice! Not that Julie was surprised—Brittany never let rivalry get in the way of friendship. Actually, many of her top competitors were also close friends. No one was sorrier than Brittany when they fell apart.

Then Ashley pushed through the crowd. "Brittany! Where have you been?" she complained, ignoring Julie completely. "This party is dead, but *dead.*"

Julie's glow evaporated as she watched Ashley preening before Brittany. Sure, Ashley hadn't even placed in the top ten this season, but she still made Julie insecure. Like Brittany, she had money, and the kind of clothes and hair that came with it. She fit in.

Brittany paused for a moment, and looked Ashley up and down. "Dead? Yes, Blaine did invite a few too many corpses. Now if you'll excuse me, I want to introduce Julie around." She slipped her arm around Julie and led her away, while Ashley's face went slack with shock.

Julie relaxed into Brittany's tan, toned arm and took another gulp of her drink. Somehow, with an alcoholic beverage in one hand and Brittany's arm around her it was easier to talk and laugh with these people in their white

Guess jeans. Her earlier shyness seemed like a distant memory as Julie told a rapt audience about the first time she rode Lady Snow.

"I was fourteen years old," she said, her eyes dreamy. "And one day I showed up at Hunterdon for a lesson and I see this beautiful gray Trakehner in one of the stalls. I couldn't believe it when Liz told me that she was mine!" Julie stopped herself before she blurted out that she had never imagined that her dad, a baker in Jersey City, would be able to scrape together enough money to buy her a horse—that was a part of the story she knew no one in this crowd would understand.

One of the trainers asked, "Liz Halstead? I forgot she was still at Hunterdon. You remember Liz, don't you, Brittany?"

"Vaguely," said Brittany. Julie recalled that Liz had been one of Brittany's early rivals. But she'd dropped out of competition just before the Grand Prix. Julie had always wondered why.

"Go on, Julie, tell us more about Lady Snow," Brittany urged her, handing her a fresh drink.

"Anyways," Julie continued, slurring her words a little, "I just knew—the first time I rode Lady Snow, and I felt those muscles, and how responsive she was, you know? Like she knew what I was *thinking* before I *thought* it."

"She's sure some horse," the trainer commented. "And she's really hitting top form at the right time. What is it? Less than a month now until the Grand Prix?"

"She seems decent enough," said Ashley, who had joined the group midway through Julie's story. "But you don't actually expect to ride a Trakehner in the Grand Prix, do you?" She added smugly, "Father bought me a Hanoverian."

Julie was crushed. She didn't have the right pants for this crowd, and she didn't have the right horse. She looked at the glass in her hand. It was empty again. If she could just have another gin and tonic, she knew she would feel better.

And then Brittany was there, with a gin and tonic in one hand, and a small cigarette in the other. A cigarette with a sweetish scent. A joint. Julie took the drink but hesitated a moment when Brittany offered her the joint. Then she saw Ashley looking at the joint, her eyes glittering with hunger. Julie took the joint. For once, someone else would be on the outside looking in.

At first Julie thought the marijuana had left her unaffected, but then she began to notice things. The pleasant haze that seemed to cover everything, the insistent beat of the music. It was as if Julie had never really *heard* the Pet Shop Boys before. The joint was passed around the circle before Ashley got hold of it. There was a comical desperation to the way Ashley drew in on the remains of the joint and Julie found herself laughing. She looked around, embarrassed, but everyone was laughing right along with her. Julie finally fit in.

"Come on, Julie, dance with me!" Brittany commanded suddenly, pulling Julie to her. As Julie started to dance, the memory she'd been trying to push away for weeks came flooding over her as intensely as if she were reliving it—reliving The Incident.

She was back in the tack room at Hunterdon, listening to an old Carpenters song, and Liz was swaying to the plaintive music. As if for a joke, Julie had started to dance with her—had put her hands on Liz's firm hips—then around her waist—and Liz had let her. But suddenly it had all turned sour. Julie, giving in to years of longing, tried to pull Liz closer, tried to sneak a knee in between Liz's sturdy thighs. Liz had pushed her away, glaring, practically frothing with shock and anger. "I can't—you're not—you don't know what you're doing. Just get away from me, kid!"

Julie's cheeks grew hot just thinking about it. The rejection had hurt, and now Liz was barely speaking to her except for that blah blah about drugs. But it wasn't the Carpenters playing now, it was Bruce Springsteen crooning on the stereo, and this wasn't Liz, it was Brittany.

Julie found herself swaying to Brittany's seductive rhythm. Brittany looked at her through half-closed eyes, and placed light hands on Julie's hips. Trembling inside, Julie clasped her hands behind Brittany's neck. She'd made a mistake with Liz, but this was no mistake because Brittany only smiled, and pulled her closer. Then suddenly, the music stopped. They both turned to see what had happened. Blaine was there, taking the record off the turntable.

"This blue-collar stuff is getting me down," he complained. "This party needs some livening *up!*"

"Blaine!" Brittany let go of Julie and hurried over to Blaine, while Julie stood there, feeling suddenly empty. Brittany kissed Blaine and they stood talking and laughing. Julie couldn't help remembering the rumors she'd heard—that Brittany and Blaine were more than first cousins. Julie didn't believe them. People just made stuff up because Brittany stayed with him in the Florida condo, and sometimes they shared a hotel room.

Julie decided she'd get another gin and tonic while Brittany and Blaine talked. She wanted to keep this good feeling going. At the bar, she caught the scent of marijuana and realized the group next to her was passing around a joint. Yes, more pot—that would help too. Julie inhaled the sweet smoke as the sounds of Boy George filtered through the room.

"Julie! There you are!" Julie turned, drink in one hand, joint in the other, as Brittany reappeared at her side. There was a feverish glitter in Brittany's eyes and she had Blaine in tow.

"Hi, Julie," he said, kissing her on the cheek as if he'd known her all her life. "You haven't been out here before, have you?" His eyes held the same strange glitter as his cousin's. "Let me show you around."

Blaine's tour took them only as far as a comfortable little room with a black leather sofa and chair, a sleek black stereo, and a glass coffee table. "My pleasure den," Blaine said with a laugh. Brittany sat on the couch and looked at Blaine expectantly. Julie's head was spinning as she watched Blaine clear off the coffee table and produce a vial filled with white powder. For a moment Julie thought it was powdered sugar, like her dad used in his bakery. Then with a shock, it hit her—cocaine!

Julie watched as Brittany and Blaine rolled up a hundred-dollar bill and snorted three lines each. Julie hesitated when they handed the bill to her. Blaine, noticing, tried to reassure her. "First time? Well, don't worry. This coke is as pure as it gets." Julie was still wavering when Brittany said in an exasperated tone, "C'mon, Julie, I thought you were cool."

Julie put down the drink and the joint she was still holding, and took the bill. Bending forward, she quickly sniffed up four lines of coke, and was rewarded with laughter and applause from Brittany and Blaine, as well as a sudden heady feeling of energy and power. She *would* have Brittany if she wanted her!

She stood up and took Brittany's hand. "I feel like dancing some more. Come on!"

"Oh, let's just stay here," Brittany replied as she pulled Julie down beside her, and the next minute her lips met Julie's in a kiss that made Julie forget the cocaine, the joint, the gin and tonic. She even forgot about Blaine sitting across from them and about Ashley, who was knocking on the door, calling, "Blaine? Brittany? Are you in there? Have you got some coke?" Still, even as she was kissing Brittany, feeling her warm body under the cashmere cowl-neck sweater, the thought flitted through Julie's mind that there was someone else she would rather have in her arms.

It was 2 A.M. when Julie stumbled back to her motel room. Brittany had invited her to spend the night, but Julie had made some feeble excuse about getting up early to exercise Lady Snow. Alone in the motel room, she cursed herself. Liz had made her feelings perfectly clear—why couldn't Julie just forget about her? She must have been crazy to pass up the chance to get it on with Brittany Fairchild!

Julie restlessly paced around the room before remembering the pills Blaine had given her when they parted. "'Ludes," he'd said, "and valium. They'll help you sleep." Julie swallowed the pills, but she was so full of cocaine and thoughts of Brittany and Liz that sleep seemed very far away. She started a list of things to do. "Buy gin," she wrote. "Have sex with Brittany." She paused. She couldn't think of what else to add. Oh yes. "Exercise Lady Snow. Win Grand Prix!" Then a wave of relaxation swept over her, and she passed out on the motel bed before she had a chance to undress.

When Julie awoke the next day, she felt fine—oh, maybe

a little draggy, but that was it. Drugs weren't so bad, after all. In fact, Julie wanted more. That warning of Liz's had just been sour grapes, she decided, since Liz was stuck giving lessons to bratty little kids now. Brittany was the one with all the trophies. Julie noticed her list from the night before and underlined, "Have sex with Brittany," with fierce decision.

By the time Julie got to the barn, the draggy feeling she'd awoken with was worse, and she was hoping that Blaine or Brittany would come by the stables that day. Finally, as Julie was trying to stop the nosebleed that had been plaguing her all morning, Blaine and Brittany appeared outside Lady Snow's stall. Julie had worried that Brittany might be angry with her for leaving the night before, but Brittany smiled at Julie and said, "Poor baby, you look like you could use a lift."

"That'd be super, Brittany." Julie nodded eagerly.

Blaine pulled out a little black bag and said, "You don't mind if we use Lady Snow's stall, do you?" The idea of involving Lady Snow made Julie uneasy somehow, but she *needed* a little boost if she was going to be able to tack up, let alone work Lady Snow over some fences. "Sure," she replied.

The trio crowded into the back of Lady Snow's stall, as the horse whinnied in alarm. Blaine pulled out a vial and a small spoon. Julie watched eagerly as he dipped the spoon into the vial and snorted its contents. He repeated the procedure three more times before handing the vial and spoon to Brittany, who did the same. By the time the vial got to Julie, she was trembling with anticipation.

After the first spoonful of cocaine, Julie felt her head clear, but she knew from last night's experience that more cocaine would make her feel even better. Julie snorted a second spoonful, and was going for a third, when Brittany grabbed the vial and said, "Slow down, honey. Leave a little for . . ." And then it happened. Julie couldn't even remember which came first—Brittany's halfhearted "Oopsy," or the sound of the vial hitting the stall floor. Before Julie could stop her, Lady Snow had snuffled up the remains of the white powder.

Julie had a sick feeling in the pit of her stomach, but Blaine and Brittany just laughed. Brittany reassured her, "Don't worry, horses love the stuff. Blizzard can't get enough!" Julie relaxed a little. After all, Brittany had won the Grand Prix on Blizzard. And besides, she told herself, it's only this once.

Julie had planned a light workout of an hour or so, but none of the jumps felt right. Was it because her thoughts were so full of Brittany? Or because Lady Snow was kind of skittish? At any rate, they both had plenty of energy, so the one hour turned into three. Even after the workout, Lady Snow still seemed restless, and Julie was hesitant to leave her. Then Brittany was there, with a handful of quaaludes and valium, showing Julie how to grind the pills into Lady Snow's bran mash. Brittany produced a second handful of pills, which she pushed toward Julie, explaining, "We're going clubbing tonight." Julie eagerly swallowed the pills, washing them down with a gulp of gin from the flask Brittany handed her.

You climbed into Brittany's Porsche and somehow you weren't surprised that Blaine was there too. The car stopped at your motel and you ran inside to shower and change. You wished you had something better to change into than your Jordache jeans and white Izod shirt. You were startled when Blaine came in before you finished dressing, but you decided not to worry about it because

Blaine was your friend now. Brittany was your friend too. They were your best friends. Best friends forever, like you used to say in high school. You wanted a gin and tonic. Then you wanted a joint. Then you wanted cocaine. Maybe you should just skip right to the cocaine? You told yourself that would be easier. You told yourself you would sniff some cocaine, and then have sex with Brittany. You thought about Liz and you told yourself not to think of Liz. You walked into the club, thinking of Liz. The strobe lights hurt your eyes. You noticed that you had another nosebleed and you hoped you wouldn't get blood on your white Izod. You saw tall fashion models wearing Gucci and Halston and you wondered what they were doing in Florida, but then you realized they were here for the coke. For Blaine's coke. Suddenly you knew everybody was after Blaine's coke, and you wondered whether Blaine really was your best friend forever, and if he would still give you coke. You wanted to ask him, but you couldn't form the words. Then you saw the vial of white powder, and you realized Blaine was your best friend forever. You crowded with him and Brittany into one of the narrow bathroom stalls, the only one where tall beautiful models weren't having sex and you took a snort of the white powder, and you realized it wasn't coke.

Julie felt a great, serene calm wash over her, like a high tide slowly creeping up a white sand beach. She felt incredibly relaxed, almost drowsy. The stall, which had seemed crowded and claustrophobic a moment ago, felt cozy now. "Say, Blaine, what is this stuff?" Julie asked. The words seemed to come out of her slowly, like cold syrup out of its container.

"This stuff?" said Blaine lazily. "Why, this is prime horse."

Julie wasn't sure she'd heard right, because she was falling into her own deep pool of calm. But it made sense when she thought about it—something that made her feel this good should definitely be called horse. Then Blaine suggested that the three of them go back to his place.

"Is that okay with you, Julie?" Brittany asked dreamily.

"Sure," Julie replied, "let's ride there on the horse."

When they arrived at the condo, Brittany led Julie upstairs and into one of the bedrooms. Then Brittany whispered, "Back in a sec, darling," and slipped out the door. Julie looked around the room, trying to avoid the images of herself reflected and re-reflected in the mirrors that covered every wall. There was still a faint voice inside Julie that was crying Liz's name, and if Julie didn't have to look at herself, it was easier to ignore that voice.

When Brittany returned she was wearing a black silk robe, with a gold monogram on the lapel. The robe clung to her every curve, revealing a body as perfect as everything else about Brittany. In her hand she had several small amber bottles. "What are—" Julie started to ask, but Brittany put a quieting finger to Julie's lips and pushed her back onto the bed. "I hope she doesn't notice it's my first time," Julie thought to herself as Brittany climbed in beside her. That was the last clear thought she had before the older girl initiated her into a sexual wonderland of pain, pleasure, and poppers. When Brittany had finished with her, Julie could barely remember her own name, much less Liz's.

The next morning, Julie felt as if her head had been stuffed full of cotton and her body ached in places that made her dread getting in the saddle that day. At the stables, Lady Snow seemed sluggish and Julie worried that the usually energetic Trakehner might be coming down with a cold. Julie had cooled her down awfully fast the day before. Then Julie noticed that Lady Snow was snuffling at her pocket, the one that held the vial Blaine had given her that morning. Julie tried to be stern with her horse. "Not while we're in training! Yesterday was an accident." But Lady Snow's snuffling had a pathetic urgency that Julie couldn't resist. The girl and her horse soon sniffed up the contents of the vial.

You snuffled around in the hay, hoping to find more of the white powder. You liked the white powder. It made you feel good. You knew you could jump higher than any of the other horses—even higher than Blizzard. You noticed that your mistress was leaving and wondered when she would be back. You liked your mistress, but you didn't like her new friends. You missed Liz. Liz would always save you an apple. Liz was your best friend forever. But you didn't want to think about Liz anymore. You wondered when your mistress would come back with more white powder. You looked over at Blizzard's stall. Blizzard always had plenty of white powder. Blizzard never had to snuffle in his stall. You wondered why you didn't get as much white powder as Blizzard did when you knew what a bad-tempered horse Blizzard was. You wanted to get out of your stall now. Your stall seemed very small suddenly. You were happy when your mistress returned with your saddle, but you were sad, because she didn't bring you any more of the white powder. Maybe Blizzard could jump higher than you after all.

Julie rushed through her workout with Lady Snow, brushing aside her nagging worries about her horse's strange behavior. Over the next few days, Julie discovered that cocaine could help her and Lady Snow get through their workout in half the usual time, and a handful of quaaludes and valium could be substituted for a thorough cool-down. And Julie needed the extra time—Brittany had two trainers and a groom for Blizzard, and wanted to spend all her free time with Julie.

Then one morning, Blaine was leaning over Julie and Brittany as they lay tangled in the sheets, chirping, "Wake up, girls! Time for my special event day breakfast—two parts crystal meth, one part cocaine, and plenty of hot coffee." The Citrus Classic—the show jumping was today! Julie couldn't believe that she had forgotten, although she had to admit that the days and nights had begun to blur together. She needed a fifth-place finish to guarantee her spot in the Grand Prix, but at the moment she wasn't sure she could even make it out of bed. Would the piles of white powder and cups of steaming black liquid on the breakfast tray Blaine was placing in front of her really help?

But once again, Blaine had the right prescription—after she'd snorted up line after line of white powder and downed cup after cup of strong black coffee, Julie not only felt like she would be able to compete that day, she *knew* that she and Lady Snow would win.

Julie hurried to the stables—she would barely have time to properly groom Lady Snow and take her through her warm-up. It had been two weeks since their last competition—a blue ribbon—and Julie wanted to leave Florida on a high note. But when Julie opened the door to Lady Snow's stall, she did a double take. She knew she hadn't been as conscientious about caring for Lady Snow lately as she should have been, but she could hardly believe that the horse in front of her *was* Lady Snow. The lids drooped over her usually alert eyes, her nostrils were red and raw, and each breath she took seemed to rattle in her chest. But then Julie remembered—she still had two vials that Blaine had given her that morning before she'd left. That would fix everything. It always did. She took them out. Blaine had even labeled them—*J* for Julie and *L* for Lady Snow. "Thank you, Blaine," said Julie fervently. Horse and girl eagerly snorted up the contents of their respective vials.

But something was wrong. Instead of perking up, Lady Snow just grew more listless. Julie had to find Blaine, but before she could go looking for him, she noticed drops of blood on her riding jacket. Damn! Not another nosebleed, not now! In a panic, she tore off the jacket and went to the tack room to wash it out. By the time Julie had finished ironing the jacket until the creases were just right, the announcer was calling her number. There was no time for Lady Snow's warm-up, no time to find Blaine. As she swung up on her horse, the certainty Julie had felt that morning vanished. She gathered the reins in her hand, fighting down something close to panic.

After all their years riding together, jumping had become instinctive for both Julie and Lady Snow. It was as if horse and rider could read each other's minds. Julie would tighten the reins almost imperceptibly, and Lady Snow would immediately adjust her stride. Julie didn't need to think about when to signal Lady Snow to start her takeoff—she felt it, and so did Lady Snow. But today was different. The connection between them had somehow been broken and Julie felt as if she were riding a stranger.

The first fence was an easy one, only four feet high, the kind of jump that Lady Snow could clear with a foot to spare. But this time, instead of feeling the mare spring up underneath her, Julie felt as if Lady Snow was barely sliding over the jump. On the way down, Julie heard a clunk. Lady Snow's back hooves had hit the top rail. Just a close call, Julie told herself, trying to psych herself up for the next jump. We'll be fine now.

Julie tightened the reins, trying to get Lady Snow to shorten her stride before the combination, but the horse continued at her own languid pace. They somehow managed to clear the first jump, but knocked over a rail on the second. Four faults. Damn! Julie looked around frantically, trying to find the next jump. She was sure it was an oxer. Too late, she remembered the water jump. Julie pulled desperately on the reins. At the last second, Lady Snow responded with a halfhearted leap. Julie thought she heard a splash. Or was it two?

"Come on, Lady Snow," Julie muttered. "Let's get it together." Lady Snow didn't even twitch her ears back. Julie had never felt so out of sync with her horse, never. It was as if Julie's brain was racing into overdrive, while Lady Snow had left hers somewhere back at the starting gate. But she had to keep going. The wall loomed ahead. Even the best jumpers can have trouble with a solid wall, Julie knew, and this particular one was the highest jump in the ring, with a sharp left-turn approach. Several riders had already taken a spill going over it.

Julie steadied herself and began to rein in Lady Snow for the approach, but Lady Snow took the turn wide and as they neared the jump, Julie could tell that their angle was all wrong. Thoughts were flashing through her brain at a million miles a second. Should she pull up now and avoid the risk of injury? Or take a chance and hope they managed to pull off that fifth-place finish? How many of Lady Snow's hooves had landed in the water? Julie was trying to replay the splashes in her head when she realized they were already in the air. For a moment, she thought they might make it. Then she pitched forward, feeling Lady Snow fall away beneath her, and hearing the heart-stopping sound of a thousand-pound horse crashing through a solid object.

Julie lay on the ground for a sickening minute, eyes tightly shut, trying to pretend it hadn't happened. Then slowly, she opened her eyes and turned toward Lady Snow. The horse lay on the ground, perfectly still. It felt like an eternity before Julie saw Lady Snow's chest rise and fall with a breath. As Julie made her way to a standing position, Lady Snow did the same. There was a polite spatter of applause, as the horse and rider exited the ring. It had not, after all, been a bad fall.

Julie cooled down the eerily calm mare, as she waited anxiously for the remaining riders to take their turns in the ring. She breathed a shaky sigh of relief when she saw that both Chase Cardwell and Isabella d'Acosta del Sol had finished out of the points as well. Julie had kept her spot in the standings. She and Lady Snow were on their way to the Grand Prix, the culmination of all their years of hard work. Yet Julie felt no joy, only an emptiness. She tried to convince herself that falls happen to every rider sooner or later, that there was nothing wrong with Lady Snow that some bran mash and a good night's sleep wouldn't fix, that everything would be okay by the time they got to the Grand Prix. But the sound of Lady Snow crashing into the wall kept echoing in her head.

Digging her hands deep in her pocket, Julie's fingers touched the vials from that morning. Maybe there'd be a little something left, something to distract her from her thoughts. When she pulled the vials out, she saw that Blaine's labels were peeling away and there was a second set of labels underneath. Julie's vial had a *C* and Lady Snow's an *H*. Julie pondered the meaning of the letters briefly, but the vials were empty, and so she tossed them away.

Brittany was waiting for her in the parking lot, leaning against her Porsche, looking cool and beautiful. "Poor baby," Brittany cooed, "let's take you home and get you fixed up."

Julie smiled weakly and slipped into the passenger seat. There she saw a blue ribbon resting on the dashboard. Julie could only manage a whispered, "Congratulations."

"Oh that," said Brittany, quickly tucking the ribbon into her bag. "You know I don't care about that, honey. All that really matters is us. You and me." Yet she radiated a satisfaction Julie could almost touch. Julie tried to feel happy for her—after all, it wasn't Brittany's fault Julie had lost the Citrus Classic.

At the condo, Blaine gave Julie a handful of pills that he promised would help her recover from her fall, but the pills only quieted the aches and pains of Julie's body. She couldn't get away from the thoughts that kept running through her head. She remembered how Lady Snow had looked standing in the stall that morning and the sickening thud as she hit the ground. She remembered the blue ribbon on Brittany's dashboard. She thought about what Liz would say if she could see Julie now. Brittany talked away as they sipped their gin and tonics and snorted some heroin, but Julie just wanted to be alone, to rest. Abruptly, Julie asked, "Would you mind if I took a nap?"

Brittany looked a little put out. "My, you must be tired!" Quickly she recovered her cool. "You know where the bed is."

Julie was asleep moments after slipping between the black satin sheets. She dreamed that she and Brittany were riding toward a jump, a wall which kept growing taller as they approached it. Brittany's horse soared high up in the sky, as if on wings, but suddenly it started to snow and Julie couldn't see the wall. She couldn't even see her horse, or herself, and she knew that she was going to crash into the wall.

Julie woke with a start, sweating and shaking. She heard noises—David Bowie on the stereo, the buzz of chatter punctuated by shrieks of laughter. It was the final party of the Florida season—Brittany's usual blowout. Julie stumbled downstairs, still in her riding clothes. She needed to find Brittany. Brittany would make the nightmare go away. At the foot of the stairs she saw Ashley, carrying a bottle of gin. "Where's Brittany?" Julie asked. A strange smile spread over Ashley's face as she pointed toward the back of the house and said, "You know where the hot tub is, don't you?"

Julie walked toward the back patio. As she got closer, she heard Blaine's voice, "Come on, Brit, I'm soooo bored." Julie stopped. Then Brittany: "She'll probably wake up any minute now." There were splashing noises. Laughter. Brittany again: "Well . . . ooooh . . . all right . . . mmm . . . don't stop." In a daze, Julie parted the fronds of a potted palm, and there were Brittany and Blaine, naked in the hot tub, deep in a passionate embrace. Automatically, Julie noted the small amber bottles strewn around the foot of the tub. Brittany saw her first. "Oh good, you're awake. Come join us."

"But I don't . . . but I'm not . . . are you?" Julie stuttered.

"Bisexual? Of course. Isn't everyone?" said Brittany with a languid wave of her hand.

Julie's head was spinning—she needed to leave that

patio, with its stench of sex and betrayal and chlorine. But even though her mind was screaming, go! her feet were rooted to the floor. She needed to get out, but there was something she needed even more, and Blaine knew exactly what it was. He leaned over the edge of the tub and started pulling an assortment of vials out of his little black bag. Just one more time, Julie told herself, then she'd be done with Brittany, with Blaine, with all of this.

Like a zombie, Julie slipped out of her clothes and into the hot tub. It was strange, she thought, how she could feel so dirty while sitting in a tub. She stared hungrily at the lines of white powder that Blaine was neatly arranging on a small mirror as he chattered away. "It's too bad about today, Julie, but I'm getting my pharmacist to cook up a little something for Lady Snow that should be just perfect for the Grand Prix."

Suddenly Julie remembered the strange markings on the vials. "Blaine, what were those letters on the vials you gave me this morning—*C* and *H*, I think it was?"

"Oh dear," Blaine replied, putting his hand to his cheek in mock horror, "did I give you one of heroin and one of cocaine? No wonder you two weren't connecting. That was awfully bad of me, wasn't it, Brit?"

"Shut up, Blaine," Brittany shot back, "I think you've said enough. It's time for Julie to have some coke."

Brittany grabbed the mirror from Blaine and pushed it at Julie. Julie reached for the mirror, but when she looked up at Brittany, there was something in Brittany's eyes that stopped her, something cold and calculating. Pictures flashed through Julie's head—Caro on crutches—Ashley begging for coke—the blue ribbon today. She didn't know yet what it all meant, but she knew something was wrong—

horribly wrong. Julie knew she had to get out of that tub, and get out now.

Before she could change her mind, Julie pulled herself out of the tub, splashing water all over the powder-laden mirror. "Julie!" exclaimed Blaine in irritation. She threw on her clothes as Brittany pleaded, "Julie, what are you doing? C'mon back in, I can make you feel good." Her shoes still untied, she fled the patio. She could hear Brittany calling after her, "Don't go! You're ruining our fun!" Ignoring the aching hunger she felt for that tantalizing white powder, she ran past the startled partiers and out of the condo. It was after midnight when she walked on blistered feet into the parking lot of her motel.

Back at the condo, her resolution had been strong, but now her hunger started to take over. Julie began to shake and twitch all over. There was an inch and a half of gin left in her bottle, and she gulped it down. She pawed frantically through the clutter on the nightstand, to see if there was anything there, anything, a 'lude, a valium, a percodan, a dexie, a bennie, a mickey, a finn, lithium, steroids, even a goddamned Tylenol. Finally, she stumbled to the bathroom, downed a bottle of cough syrup, and ate a tube of Sensodyne toothpaste. It wasn't much, but it got her through the night.

The next morning, a twitching, shaking Julie hitched up the trailer and led a twitching, shaking Lady Snow into it. As Julie drove north, the ache got worse and worse. By the time she hit the New Jersey Turnpike, she was starting to calculate how quickly she could get Lady Snow settled in at Hunterdon, and where she could find Brittany and Blaine.

At Hunterdon, Julie stumbled out of her car and rubbed

her eyes. Everything was just as she'd left it—bucolic and peaceful. Only Julie had changed. She felt as if she'd aged a hundred years.

"Juuuulieeee," cooed a voice behind her. Julie jumped a foot, and turned, twitching. Brittany and Blaine had pulled into the driveway and were getting out of Blaine's BMW. As they approached, Brittany shook her head and purred, "Poor Julie, she doesn't look well."

"Not well at all," Blaine chimed in, opening his black bag.

Julie was shaking all over. She watched Blaine slowly undoing the buckles as if she were hypnotized. She had no awareness of anything else in the world but that black bag. Then, she heard a gasp. "Julie!"

She turned, slowly, reluctant to let the bag out of her sight. Liz was looking at her, eyes wide with horror. Julie knew she hadn't been eating well, and that she hadn't slept in two days, and that she was still wearing yesterday's riding clothes, which were now spattered with dried blood from numerous nosebleeds, but did she really look *that* bad?

"Liz!" Brittany exclaimed, "It's been ages, darling. You're looking . . . older."

"And you, Brittany, you haven't changed a bit, have you?" Liz responded angrily, gesturing toward Julie.

"Long time no see, Lizzie," Blaine said. "What step are you on now? Forty-three?"

Julie's head was awhirl with confusion—what was the connection between Liz and Brittany? What was Blaine talking about? And when could she get some coke?

"I want you two out of here—and away from Julie," Liz said fiercely.

"But Julie wants to come with us," Brittany responded.

"She doesn't need you—you, your blow, or your bag of bisexual tricks!" Liz shot back.

Brittany laughed. "Oh, Lizzie, you're just as boring out of bed as you were in it. Don't be too sure you know what Julie wants and doesn't want. I can tell you firsthand—Julie likes to have fun."

Julie gasped. Had Brittany slept with Liz? Was Liz in love with Brittany? And was Liz really boring in bed?

"Julie doesn't need your kind of fun," Liz snapped.

"Julie's all grown up now," Brittany said sharply. "She can decide for herself. Come on Julie. Let's get going."

Julie looked back and forth between Liz and Brittany, comparing Brittany's perfectly groomed blond hair to Liz's tousled black curls, Brittany's pampered slenderness to Liz's sturdy muscularity, Brittany's blue eyes with their feverish glitter to Liz's clear, calm sea-foam green eyes. Julie wanted to stay with Liz, but did she have the strength to say goodbye to that little black bag?

As Julie stood there, frozen, a high-pitched whinny split the air. Everyone turned toward Lady Snow's trailer. Now there was the sound of hooves, thudding against the door. And when Liz opened the trailer, there was Lady Snow, frothing at the mouth and rolling her eyes, begging Julie for help—for relief.

"She trusted me and this is what I did to her," Julie realized. Her numbed brain struggled to grasp the enormity of what she'd done—and what she had to do now.

"Don't worry, Julie. Blaine's got something in his bag for Lady Snow. Now what's it going to be?" Brittany said with a confident smile as she motioned Blaine toward the horse trailer.

Julie stared at the ground. "I—I want you both to leave now. I'm staying here." Her voice was barely audible, but she'd said it.

For a moment, Brittany was speechless. Then her face turned an ugly shade of red, and as she climbed into the BMW, she screeched, "Fine! But I hope you don't think that you and that mangy Trakehner of yours are going to win the Grand Prix. Brittany is going to win the Grand Prix! Brittany *always* wins the Grand Prix!" Julie could still hear Brittany ranting as Blaine peeled out of the parking lot.

As Julie watched the BMW drive away, she dissolved into sobs. "I can't do it, Liz! I'm not strong enough!"

Liz's arms were around her. "You *can* do it, Julie."

"You don't understand," Julie wailed. "You don't know what this is like!"

Liz looked intently into Julie's tearstained face. "But I do understand, because when I was nineteen, I went through exactly the same thing—Brittany, Blaine, the drugs, all of it."

Julie could hardly believe what she was hearing.

"Halfway through the season, Brittany and I were neck and neck in the standings. We were in Florida. I was young, naive, and lonely—the perfect target for someone like her. By the time we left Florida, I would have sold my horse for a fix, and my horse would have done the same with me. And we're not the only ones—Brittany's gone through more promising riders than you or I have gone through saddle pads."

"Is that why you never rode in the Grand Prix?" Julie asked as she finally began to realize the answers to questions long unasked.

"I left the circuit to go to Betty Ford. I managed to put together a new life for myself, but I . . . I never got up the courage to return to the old one. Most don't. Brittany's chosen a game where the odds are all stacked in her favor, and so far, she's won every time. But you and Lady Snow, I think you two have something special. What do you say, kid? Are you going to be the one to beat her?"

Julie took a deep, shaky breath. "I'm ready to try."

For two solid days, Liz stayed in the locked stall with Julie and Lady Snow, as the two sweated the poisons out of their system. When it was over, Lady Snow gobbled sugar cube after sugar cube, and so did Julie.

"Liz, I don't know how to thank you," Julie said, eyes shining.

"You don't have to thank me. Don't you know I'd do anything for you?" Liz said gruffly.

"Anything?" Julie ventured, putting her hand on Liz's shoulder. Liz drew back from Julie's touch.

"What is it, Liz? Why do you always pull away from me? Don't you care for me?"

"Of course I do—I've loved you since you were eleven!"

Liz loved her! Julie couldn't believe she was finally hearing those words after so many years of dreaming about them.

But Liz was still talking, her voice strained and tense. "But I can't—we can't ever do anything. For me, sex is all tied up with Brittany, drugs, and hot tubs. And I just know that if—if I have sex again, I'll slip back into all of that."

For an instant, Julie's heart plummeted. Would she never be free of Brittany and her trail of destruction? Then she reminded herself that only two days before she'd been a slave to cocaine. Liz had helped Julie break free of her addiction—now Julie knew it was up to her to help Liz break free of the past.

Julie encircled Liz in a firm yet tender embrace. "I'm not going to let Brittany take riding away from me, and I won't let her take you either."

At first the older woman stiffened, then she struggled, but finally she relaxed into Julie's embrace. Julie slowly tightened her arms until their two bodies were pressed against each other. Liz shuddered all over, but it was no longer with fear, only desire. The two slid down into a pile of hay where they discovered that when two people truly love and respect each other, they don't need poppers to experience a sexual wonderland of pain and pleasure.

Only a few weeks later, Julie found herself astride Lady Snow, waiting to enter the ring at the Grand Prix. She knew that physically they'd both recovered, and were as fit as they'd been before they ever met Brittany, Blaine, and Blizzard. But had she and Lady Snow recovered their harmony and trust? Would they be able to find their old confidence?

Julie almost regretted asking Liz to watch from the stands, but this was something she and Lady Snow needed to do by themselves.

Julie looked up at the scoreboard and saw that Brittany's time was still the one to beat. She hadn't watched her ride the course. She thought she was strong enough now to resist Brittany—but she was afraid.

"Julie!"

It was Brittany's voice, commanding Julie to turn around. Julie turned.

Brittany stood below her, still in riding clothes. Her hair

was golden, her eyes were blue, her skin was tanned. She was still Brittany—still beautiful and seductive.

Julie took a deep breath. Seeing Brittany was kicking up a lot of stuff for her. Memories were rushing over her, some of them good, most of them bad.

"Think you're going to win today, Julie?" The question was a taunt.

Julie answered slowly. "I don't know, Brittany. I just do the best I can and try to stay free of chemical substances. That makes me a winner already, in a way."

Brittany's lip curled. "Can that bullshit! This isn't one of your meetings. I just have something I want to tell you."

Julie remembered how she used to quail before that curled lip, which always meant Brittany was disappointed in her. But now she wasn't quailing. Instead she was listening to something new in Brittany's voice, something that Julie hadn't heard before. Suddenly Julie realized what it was—it was fear!

"You're a loser," Brittany was saying. "I played you. I played your precious Liz. I played them all! Nobody beats Brittany!"

Julie wasn't paying attention. She was noticing for the first time that Brittany's blond hair had dark roots. Brittany's blue eyes were riddled with tiny red lines. Brittany's tanned face was etched with faint wrinkles. And how was it she'd never noticed before that Brittany's eyebrows had been singed off from freebasing?

"I can have anybody I want, man or woman! All I have to do is snap my fingers!" Brittany tried to snap her fingers, but her hands were trembling so hard she couldn't.

Julie heard her number being called over the PA. "Goodbye, Brittany," she said, gently clucking to Lady Snow.

"I'm a winner," Brittany called after her, her voice high with hysteria. "Do you hear me? Brittany Fairchild is the winner!"

Julie realized Brittany had no more power over her—she felt no fear, only pity. Brittany still didn't understand that when you play with drugs, nobody wins. Julie smiled at Liz up in the stands, put Brittany out of her mind, and took a deep breath. She brought Lady Snow into a balanced, rhythmic canter and headed into the ring, knowing that all they had to do now was take life one fence at a time.

Ride to Freedom

Jennie glanced at the clock. Jeb and his friends would be arriving soon for their poker night, and dinner had to be ready when they got there. Preparing the meal in the modern yellow kitchen with its avocado appliances should have been fulfilling; at least that was what Jennie had read in that *Good Housekeeping* article on "Decorating Tips for the Self-Actualized Housewife." So why was it that each time she looked out the window and saw Firebird moving restlessly about the paddock, the yellow walls of the kitchen seemed to close in on her? Jennie wasn't sure why, but she had to get away from the ranch, if only for a little while. "I won't be gone long," she promised herself, throwing down her oven mitt. She ran outside, quickly saddled up the eager filly, and urged Firebird out the gate.

In the year since she'd married Jeb, she'd tried to get used to her new role as "wife," to be a gracious hostess to his friends. But she still cringed at their crude talk, still grimaced at the tobacco juice she had to scrub out of the rugs when, after a few six packs, they would inevitably miss the jug. She knew she would never feel at ease with "the boys." Would she ever feel comfortable with Jeb?

Jennie slowed Firebird to a walk as the path wound its way through a grove of majestic Oregonian pines. Her thoughts drifted back to the time before her marriage—the time when she had first felt like an outsider. After high school graduation, the group of friends she'd made her first summer at Girl Scout camp had begun to drift apart. Some of the girls had gotten married, while others had taken jobs in offices where there were eligible bachelors. Jennie had puzzled them all by taking a job as a riding instructor back at their old Girl Scout camp. Jennie loved initiating young girls into the joys of horses, but grew tired of her girlfriends' constant refrain, "Better watch out, or you'll end up an old maid."

Then she'd met Jeb in town one day, she buying oats, he buying supplies for his 500-acre spread. When he'd shown an interest in her, Jennie had felt a sense of relief, as if she were finally in step with the rest of the world. Within a month, they were engaged. Her girlfriends were like sisters again, helping her do her hair and pick out new outfits. The weeks leading up to her wedding were a happy whirlwind. People said she was radiant on her wedding day.

Afterward, Jeb had insisted that Jennie trade in her job at the camp for full-time work as his wife. During the long, lonely days on the ranch that followed, Jennie began to wonder if she and Jeb had anything at all in common. Even in bed, she couldn't help shrinking from Jeb's physical demands, from the touch of his heavy, work-hardened hands.

Jennie spurred Firebird up the mountain, as if to escape from her memories. But like hungry bears they chased after her—she remembered all the times she had tried to share her doubts and unhappiness with her girlfriends, only to have them respond as if she were betraying them.

"Jeb Hoskins was the most eligible bachelor in town. How can you complain about a fine catch like that?"

"That ranch of his seems to do awfully well. Is that a new outfit?"

"Maybe if you spent a little less time on that horse of yours and a little more time paying attention to your man, you wouldn't be having these problems."

Less time on Firebird! Jennie had loved the filly from the moment she'd first laid eyes on her, the summer she turned sixteen. She had arrived at Girl Scout camp eager as ever for two months of hiking, camping, swimming, and riding—especially riding! But her friends were interested only in planning forays into town to meet boys.

Jennie had felt miserable and alone, until the morning Barb Hanson, the strict, athletic camp director, had arrived leading Firebird. When Jennie saw the filly, part appaloosa, part quarter horse, her coat a beautiful deep brown with a sprinkling of white across her hindquarters, she felt she had found a soul mate. Barb's iron jaw had relaxed into a smile as she announced that the older girls would be able to "explore some new terrain" on the fiery filly.

And explore new terrain they had. It was on a camping trip, with Barb and a few of the older girls, that Jennie had glimpsed the fabled mustangs. Jennie could remember hearing about these horses since she was a girl, a herd of wild mustangs that roamed the dense forests of the craggy Oregon hills.

It had been just after dawn that Jennie was awakened by Firebird's whinnying. She went to soothe the horse and was rewarded by the magical sight of a band of mustangs thundering through the valley below. Jennie had watched until the horses disappeared from view. Only then did she notice Barb's presence by her side. "Beautiful, aren't they?" Barb had whispered reverently.

Ever since then, Jennie had awoken to dim memories of the herd thundering through her dreams. Those dreams had persisted right up until the day she'd married Jeb. That was when the herd had abandoned her. Or had she abandoned them? Jennie only knew that she missed them as much as if their presence in her life had been as real as Firebird's.

As if sensing her mistress's thoughts, Firebird whickered, a low, affectionate noise. The horse had all an appaloosa's beauty and spirit, mated with the keen intelligence of a quarter horse. What would married life have been like without Firebird? Jennie shuddered at the thought.

The filly had been an unexpected wedding present from Barb. When Jennie told Barb she was leaving to be married, she had been shocked to see a tear trickle down the tough camp director's leathery cheek. Later, when Jennie was saying her own tearful goodbye to Firebird, Barb had told her the horse was hers.

Barb. Life brought funny changes. Once Jennie had been Barb's employee, but in the year after she'd left the camp, Barb had fallen on hard times. First a timber company had bought up the land Barb had leased for her camp. Then came the hospitalizations, as the years of smoking caught up with Barb. Finally, there was nothing more the doctors could do for her. With only half a lung left, Barb was released from the hospital—little more than her gritty determination keeping her alive. With heartbreaking humility, she had accepted Jennie's offer of a little room off the stable. Maybe she'd guessed how Jennie had to beg before Jeb would consent to let her take in her old camp counselor.

Jennie's thoughts came back to the present with a jolt and she looked around. Firebird had stopped of her own accord, and was peacefully munching wildflowers. They had reached the point where the forest thickened. Jennie longed to penetrate its mysterious vastness, but something had always held her back. With a sigh, she gathered the reins in her hand, and turned back toward the ranch. She hoped she'd have enough time to bring Barb the little bit of food she could choke down these days, before she finished making the men's supper.

When Jennie rode into the paddock, she noted with relief that Jeb's pickup was not yet back. Hurriedly, she heated up a bowl of broth on the stove. She threw the half-scrubbed potatoes into the oven and set the steaks to sizzling, then took the broth out to the little room by the stables. Barb was sleeping fitfully under an old horse blanket, each breath a painful rasp.

As Jennie entered the room, Barb stirred. "Jennie?" she managed to wheeze, before a spasm of coughs shook her.

"I'm here, Barb," replied Jennie, covering her sorrow with a smile for Barb's sake.

When the coughing had subsided, Barb engaged in their nightly ritual. "I think I'm improving. I won't be a burden to you much longer."

"You're looking better, Barb, but you can't leave—I'd miss your company too much." Jennie sat down on the edge of the bed, and started to feed Barb. But Barb took the spoon from her. "You go on, I know it's Jeb's poker night. I don't want to get him all riled up at you." Feebly, she began to spoon the broth into her mouth.

Jennie watched, biting her lip. It broke her heart to see the proud old woman tremulously dripping soup all over the horse blanket. But her own anxieties drove her back to the kitchen.

Jennie rushed to the stove, but it was too late—the steaks were overdone. Jeb liked them practically raw. A rumble of voices told her the men were arriving. She closed her eyes, trying to will her stomach out of the knot it was tightening into, but her eyes snapped open when someone slapped her on the backside.

"Wake up, honey!" It was one of her husband's friends—she couldn't remember his name—they all looked alike to her. "You've got hungry men to feed!" Thrusting a six-pack at her, he left the kitchen. Jennie looked around in despair, but there was no escape.

That night, the talk was all about the mustangs.

"A fellow from the logging crew was telling me that they saw those mustangs again last week," one of the men said, speaking as he chewed.

"That's the third time this month," another man added.

Jennie remembered when years would pass between sightings, but recently loggers had moved into the area, making their mark on formerly pristine forests. Now that the hillsides were being cleared of trees, Jeb and the boys had high hopes of capturing the herd.

"Say, Jeb, I wouldn't mind breaking a couple of those horses," called a bearded man on Jennie's right.

"Some of those mustangs just won't break. Sometimes there's nothing left to do but shoot 'em," Jeb returned.

"But if you can't break them, why not just let them go instead of shooting them?" Jennie had found herself wondering aloud.

Jeb had rolled his eyes as the men burst out laughing. The man who had slapped her called out to Jeb, "What's going on here? Your wife one of those women's libbers?" He then turned to Jennie. "Don't you know that you can get fifty cents a pound from the dog food factory?"

Tears sprang to Jennie's eyes at the thought. Why couldn't the men leave the horses free to wander the Oregon hills as they had done for generations?

That night, while she slept, the mustangs returned to Jennie's dreams. She was riding Firebird bareback through the forests. Shots rang out around them but could not touch them. They rode into a clearing and there they were—the band of mustangs. But no, it was a troop of Girl Scouts, gathered around a campfire, hands joined. The girls opened their mouths to begin a song, but instead they all put a pinch of tobacco between their cheek and gum. Jennie then saw that it was not a troop of Girl Scouts sitting there; it was Jeb and the boys. She tried to call out to Jeb as he raised a rifle and aimed it at Firebird, but could only clutch at her throat, realizing she had no voice. A shot rang out and Jennie awoke covered in a cold sweat.

Even though she knew it had been a dream, Jennie couldn't stop herself from springing out of bed and rushing to the barn to check on Firebird. Then, as if she were still dreaming, she mounted the filly. Firebird danced lightly back and forth, enjoying the unaccustomed feeling of bare flesh and the silk of Jennie's peignoir on her back, rather than the unyielding leather of the saddle.

They rode out of the paddock, woman and horse moving as one, sharing the same desire to leave the fences and buildings behind and wander among the trees. When they reached the point where the forest thickened and she had always turned back, Jennie urged Firebird on. The scent of pine was like wine to both woman and horse.

Jennie leaned forward, her auburn hair whipping in the wind, her silk peignoir fluttering behind her. The smooth rhythm of Firebird's withers and crest rising and falling hypnotized her. Firebird's mane whipped her face, making her blood tingle. The horse cantered faster and faster over the narrow path that wound through the dense forest. Jennie wanted to cry out with the ecstasy she felt growing inside her.

Suddenly, they burst into a hidden clearing, and a fountain of bright sunlight poured over them as they raced across a sea of waving green grass and tiny blue wild flowers. For an instant, Jennie's sun-dazzled eyes glimpsed something her mind could not comprehend—there was another horse, coal black, disappearing into the forest at the far end of the clearing, and on its back a woman, riding like an Amazon, naked and barebacked. Jennie stopped to catch her breath, rubbing her eyes in disbelief. Then the horse reappeared, riderless. Had she only imagined the woman?

Another horse appeared, and another. Slowly horse after horse emerged from the forest until Jennie and Firebird were surrounded by a herd of horses. The mustangs! Jennie shivered with excitement. Was she dreaming again? No, the clearing, the horses—this time they were real. Jennie gazed at the herd—sturdy, compact horses of all colors with rough, ungroomed manes and eyes gleaming with intelligence—eyes that seemed to say, "We know you mean us no harm." The next moment the horses were in motion, running like the wind, and then they were gone.

Jennie and Firebird were alone in the clearing and it was

time to return to the ranch. On the ride back, it occurred to Jennie that it was her responsibility as Jeb's wife to tell him what she had seen—a duty she found even more unwelcome than Jeb's nightly invasions of her womanhood.

At breakfast Jeb was gruff, and Jennie was unusually quiet as a battle waged within her. Did she owe no loyalty to the wild and free horses? But what of the vows she had taken before God and man—she had vowed her first loyalty to Jeb, hadn't she? Then Jeb spoke up, interrupting her thoughts.

"Want to tell me why you had to go for a ride this morning when you should have been making me my breakfast?"

"Jeb, I . . ."

"God knows I've been patient, but I'm hard at work on the ranch all day. All I ask is three meals a day, on time—and that the house be nice and clean, and my clothes washed and ironed—and that you're nice to my buddies—and that when the kids start coming, you take good care of them. I'll do the rest. Maybe we should just sell that filly—all the feed she takes."

"Oh Jeb! No!"

"Hey, you promised to love, honor, and obey *me,* not that horse. A new pickup would be more useful—"

Jennie spoke quickly, out of a mixture of duty and fear. "Jeb, I saw the mustangs."

It was a hollow victory to see Jeb forget about selling Firebird as he eagerly questioned her and she described for him where she had seen the horses. Jennie wondered miserably if she'd done the right thing. The echoing voices from the past—her parents, her girlfriends, her teachers—told her yes, but her heart said no.

That night, when she took Barb her broth, Jennie told Barb about the mustangs and what she had done. After a long moment, Barb spoke.

"You did the right thing, Jennie," she said. "Jeb's your husband. Anyway, somebody's going to catch those mustangs sooner or later. Freedom like that can never last."

Jennie felt a little better, until she went back to Barb's room to fetch the bowl she'd forgotten. Barb was staring out the window at the distant hills, tears streaming down her face.

That night, Jennie dreamed again. Again she was in the forest, but this time she felt the cold steel of the rifle in her own hands as she made her way into the clearing. Behind her walked a phalanx of Girl Scouts, each with a rifle in her hands. As she entered the clearing, the mustangs were grazing peacefully. Jennie raised the rifle to her shoulder and fixed her sights on the center of the herd. Through the rifle sight, she watched as the herd parted and Firebird emerged. Jennie smiled. As she bent to lay down the rifle, she heard shots ring out from behind her and saw the horses fall.

Jennie awoke, sobbing, and ran to the window. She could just make out Jeb and the boys through the cloud of dust raised by their horses as they went off in search of the mustangs. Jennie sat all day by the window, while dinner slow-cooked in the crockpot. When Jeb returned that evening and reported that they'd had no luck, Jennie hoped her face did not betray the flood of relief she felt.

The next few days, when the men went in search of the herd, Jennie would ramble around the big ranch house, vacuuming the shag carpeting, sewing appliqué flowers on the curtains, trying desperately to find things to do to take her mind off the mustangs. Once, in her distraction, she let the dinner overcook. That night she felt a strange satisfaction when she put a lump of charred meat on Jeb's plate—she would not fuel his search for the mustangs. The next night she made quiche. These small rebellions only brought momentary relief. Her nights were plagued by the same dream over and over—Jennie carrying the rifle, the mustangs, Firebird, and then the shots. She began to avoid sleeping altogether.

She longed for peace. One night, Jennie went out to the barn, hoping her old camp counselor could provide some measure of comfort, but when she looked down at the frail body under the horse blanket, she knew she could not bring more pain into Barb's life. She was Barb's protector now. Jennie looked at the steaming bowl of broth in her hands. She nourished Barb. She had saved Barb. If only she could save the mustangs.

That night, after Jeb had satisfied himself while Jennie lay passively beneath him, she struggled to stay awake, her thoughts in a turmoil. She had to do something—something more than burning dinner and making quiche—but what? Finally, she could fight off sleep no longer, and with sleep came the dream.

But this time it was different. Again Jennie led the army of Girl Scouts into the clearing. Again she aimed her rifle and the herd parted to reveal Firebird. But this time, when Jennie went to put down her rifle, she saw that it was not a rifle at all. Instead it was an earthenware bowl, filled with cool water. She set the bowl down and Firebird came and drank. Then there were bowls everywhere and the herd was drinking. The Girl Scouts slipped astride the horses, but when Jennie looked again, she saw that they were not girls, but women. Before Jennie's eyes the women and horses became one, like some beautiful creatures out of Greek mythology.

The next morning, when Jennie awoke, she felt a sense of peace and purpose that she had not known since before her marriage. She managed to slip out of the house and onto Firebird before Jeb was even awake. Firebird seemed to know which direction to take before Jennie had touched the reins. With a skill almost uncanny, Firebird picked her way swiftly over roots and boulders, in and out of gullies, skirting patches of poison sumac, but always heading for the clearing. When they arrived, the clearing was empty, but both woman and horse detected a scent in the air which meant the herd had not been gone long. Senses quivering, they waited. Jennie realized she must have drifted off, because when she opened her eyes, they were there. The horses looked at her with the same unspoken trust they had the first time and it was like a knife through Jennie's heart. She whispered brokenly, "I'm sorry. I'm sorry."

"They know," came a throaty whisper from behind Jennie. Jennie twisted in her saddle, and for an instant she thought she was looking at one of the woman-horses from her dream. It felt no less dreamlike when Jennie realized that this was the woman she had glimpsed that fateful day in the clearing. As she stared, open-mouthed, the woman seemed to shimmer and dissolve. The shock and sleeplessness caught up with her, and Jennie slid from her saddle in a dead faint.

Gradually Jennie returned to consciousness and became aware of the woman bending over her and the poultice of herbs the woman was applying to Jennie's head. In her fevered state, Jennie made a convulsive effort to sit up.

"Wait." The woman pressed her back into the cradle of the sun-baked earth with her large, capable hands. "You've been hurt. Rest. We will take care of you."

Jennic sank back into the hillock as she remembered her wild ride with Firebird and her fall. She struggled up again, exclaiming, "Firebird! The mustangs!"

"They're fine." The woman smiled. Her warm brown eyes gleamed in her warm brown face. "And your horse is making friends." With one muscular arm she hoisted Jennie up, like a mother bear with its cub. Jennie saw with relief that Firebird was cropping grass several yards away, in a small herd of horses. "The herd," Jennie said drowsily. "Are they yours?"

"Ours?" Jennie could sense the indulgent amusement in the woman's response. "We share the valley with them. Sometimes we ride them. They give us their dung for our herb garden. They are our friends."

Who was this woman? And whom did she mean by "we"? Overcome by the bewildering events and the pungent scent from the poultice mixed with the pungent scent of the mysterious woman, Jennie fell asleep once more.

When she awoke, it was again in unfamiliar surroundings. She gingerly sat up on a woven straw pallet and saw she was on the porch of a ramshackle old farmhouse, in a valley she had never known existed. The yard in front of the farmhouse was covered with beds of greens of all descriptions, from lettuce and chard to cilantro and chives. From the windows of the farmhouse hung swaths of loosely woven cloth dyed turquoise and lavender. At the other end of the porch, a woman was intently molding the clay that spun before her on a potting wheel. The woman was surrounded by bowls, dishes, and mugs of all description. Hearing the rustle of the pallet, she looked up and smiled at Jennie.

"Hi!" she said cheerfully. "How are you feeling? Do you want a cup of tea, or water or something?" She reminded Jennie of the friendly Avon ladies, except that her blond hair was a bit unkempt, and she seemed to be wearing a burlap sack.

"How did I get here?" asked Jennie faintly.

"Lisa Moondaughter brought you—she said you'd had a fall from your horse. Gee, I hope you're okay. Does your head still hurt?" She sat beside Jennie on the straw pallet, looking at her with friendly concern.

"Who—who did you say brought me here?" asked Jennie.

"Lisa Moondaughter," repeated the blond woman. "Well, that's not exactly her real name—see, we keep our first names but discard our last names as a protest against the Patriarchy. We choose last names that really *say* something about *who we are.*"

"I see," breathed Jennie, her eyes widening in astonished admiration at this bold move. She wondered what name she would take if she could discard Jeb's last name. Windrider? Horsegroomer?

"For instance, I'm Kimberly Claysmoother," the friendly blonde explained, "because I make most of the pottery. Look." She handed Jennie a plate and Jennie stared openmouthed, unconsciously running her fingers over the genitalia-inspired curves. "But what if there are two people who want to be Claysmoothers?" she asked.

"Actually, that did come up," Kimberly Claysmoother admitted. "Dolores wanted to be Clayspinner, but after we discussed it for a couple hours at our weekly community meeting, really talking out all the issues it brought up for everyone, she decided she'd be pretty happy with Potholder." Kimberly Claysmoother's eyes were dreamy as she remembered the womanly energy at the meeting, and the exhausted look on Dolores's face as she exclaimed, "I really don't give a shit anymore, just call me Potholder."

"That sounds wonderful," said Jennie enviously, thinking to herself, Jeb and I never bring up issues with each other. But her mind moved on, as more questions bubbled up to her eager lips. "How did you come here? How many of you are there? How do you survive, just eating greens?"

"I see you're feeling better," said a warm, husky voice. Jennie looked up and saw Lisa Moondaughter. Her brown eyes looked at Jennie with a gaze as liquid and warm as chocolate syrup, and Jennie's heart was like ice cream, melting beneath it. Lisa Moondaughter had clothed her statuesque beauty in a loosely woven tuniclike garment dyed a rich loamy color, but Jennie remembered the shape and look of the womanly swells it concealed, and her breath quickened.

"Come. I will show you the farm," Lisa Moondaughter beckoned.

"I'd like that," said Jennie.

Lisa Moondaughter took Jennie's hand and pulled her up off the straw pallet. Jennie felt a current of electricity flowing through her, but realized it was only Lisa Moondaughter's womanly power dizzying her with its strength.

"First, we'll stop by the garden and give you a new dressing," said Lisa Moondaughter, leading the way into the sun-drenched yard. She stooped among the plants and her deft fingers plucked several different herbs, which she laid gently on Jennie's bruised forehead with her strong hands.

"What kind of herbs are these?" Jennie asked, then laughing at herself, apologized, "I guess I'm full of questions right now."

"Don't apologize for your curiosity," said Lisa Moondaughter as she deftly tied a piece of loosely woven purple fabric around Jennie's head to hold the herbs in place. Every time her warm brown fingers brushed Jennie's head, Jennie felt shivers run up and down her spine. "It's only natural that all this should feel strange to you," Lisa Moondaughter continued, "after living so long in the world of men."

"That's the funny thing, though," Jennie said wonderingly. "It's all so . . . so different, yet in a way, it feels more familiar than anyplace I've ever been."

Lisa Moondaughter said nothing, but gave Jennie a slow smile of understanding. She led Jennie behind the farmhouse and Jennie caught her breath at the vista of women spread before her—women of all shapes, sizes, and colors, in all stages of dress and undress, engaged in plowing, weaving, firing pottery, or just sitting under trees doing yoga.

"It began when I was in law school," said Lisa Moondaughter. "I became sickened by the justice created by men, for men. I saw all around me what men had made of the world—pollution, racism, poverty. And the rents in New York were skyrocketing . . ."

"New York!" exclaimed Jennie. "I've always wanted to see New York."

"It's a wasteland," said Lisa Moondaughter simply. She put her hand briefly on the shoulder of a woman weaving. "One of our working-class sisters," she murmured to Jennie, then continued her story. "I came here with my lover—this farm belonged to her family—and with us came a small band of women who wanted to return to Mother Earth and let her nurture them, away from men."

"Then you're all—" Jennie choked on the word, her cheeks reddening.

"We are all women-identified women," said Lisa Moondaughter bluntly.

Jennie turned away for a moment, to hide the unexpected excitement this revelation caused, and surveyed the farm. "How idyllic this seems!" she exclaimed. With her back to Lisa Moondaughter, she was unable to see the tremor that shook the woman's habitual impassiveness as she gazed at Jennie, whose body was outlined against the blue sky, and whose auburn curls were set aflame by the late afternoon sun. But when Jennie turned around, Lisa Moondaughter was again as serene and immobile as a Henry Moore sculpture.

"And you can support yourselves like this, living off the land?"

"Well, not quite," Lisa Moondaughter admitted. "Perhaps in a few years we will live the dream of complete independence from the Patriarchy, but right now we earn money selling our pottery and weaving at women's music festivals and peace fairs. This we use to buy necessities we can't make, like sea salt, wheat germ, and tofu."

"Tofu?" said Jennie wonderingly.

Lisa Moondaughter led her to a barrel by the barn and, after removing the cover, stepped aside to let Jennie peer in. Jennie gazed at the bloated white blocks that looked like rotting cheese, floating in the water. As she exclaimed at the sight, a sullen-faced woman, her hair cropped short, approached, carrying a loosely woven straw basket.

"Excuse me," she grunted. "I'm on tofu-gathering duty."

"Jennie, this is Heather," Lisa Moondaughter introduced them as the woman began to scoop up the chunks of tofu.

"Heather . . . ?" Jennie questioned.

"Just Heather," said Heather shortly. "Isn't it enough to be named after a plant? How much more natural do I have to be?"

"Heather," said Lisa Moondaughter gently, "hadn't you better see Judy Leafdripper for some moonforce tea?"

Heather's shoulders slumped in resignation. "I guess I could try it," she muttered as she hurried away. "What I wouldn't give for a Midol."

"You all get along so well!" marveled Jennie. She stage-whispered, "Heather has cramps, huh?"

"It is her time of the month." Lisa Moondaughter smiled. For a moment they stood by the tofu barrel, sharing the eternal bond of womanly experience.

The women were slowly drifting toward the house now, talking among themselves, wiping dirt from their hands, smiling and calling greetings to each other. It made Jennie feel she had returned to Girl Scout camp—a woman-centered world, where nature was important. It was hard to believe that the joy she had experienced there was again hers—yet not hers. With a sigh she turned to Lisa Moondaughter.

"You have to go," Lisa Moondaughter said, voicing Jennie's reluctant thoughts.

"I don't want to, but Jeb—that's my husband—he'll be waiting for me." Lisa Moondaughter stared mutely as Jennie tried to find the words to explain why this had to be. "My place is with him . . ." Jennie began, but found herself trailing off, wondering where those words had come from. "We can't all live in this utopia!" she finally said in desperation.

"You can. Join with us." Lisa Moondaughter moved almost imperceptibly toward Jennie. "With me."

Jennie gasped as she gazed at Lisa Moondaughter in the growing twilight. "I've watched you," Lisa Moondaughter continued. "I've seen the way you ride your horse, so wildly through the forest. Since my lover died . . ."

"Your lover died?" interrupted Jennie curiously.

"Yes. Of E. coli she caught at the Michigan Womyn's Music Festival on a selling expedition." Jennie watched helplessly as a dark cloud of sadness passed over Lisa Moondaughter's face, like a shadow over the sea. "Bad hummus," she continued after a moment. "After her death I felt as though I'd turned to stone. I spent hours riding the wild horses, traveling with the herd. I thought nothing could ever stir me again—until I saw you."

The magnetic force that had been building between them reached its peak at the end of Lisa Moondaughter's speech. Jennie and Lisa Moondaughter gazed at each other, each finding what she was looking for in the other's eyes. They fell to the soft green grass by the tofu barrel, their bodies intertwined in the timeless dance of woman love. The earth shifted and mountains came together. Oceans of salty nectar flowed. As one, the women were shaken by tremors, as if the herd of wild horses were thundering through them.

"You can share my straw pallet," Lisa Moondaughter planned, as they lay curled together sometime later. "I will teach you how to weave, and we will ride with the herd—"

"I want you to teach me everything," said Jennie,

stretching luxuriously. Even the ecstasy she had felt astride Firebird paled in comparison to the fulfillment that she and Lisa Moondaughter had just shared.

"We will grow old together," Lisa Moondaughter whispered in her ear. "When you are sick, I will care for you. And I will never, never let you eat the hummus."

Sick old women! Jennie sat up as if she'd heard a rifle shot. How could she have forgotten about Barb? What would Barb do without her? And what about her vows to Jeb? Did they mean nothing? The chorus of voices, which had been silenced for this blissful interlude, were back with a vengeance. All the rest of her life could not be washed away in the blink of an eye, not even by Lisa Moondaughter's womanly juices.

"I must go," she said in a voice that trembled. "The ranch . . ." She groped for her clothes, keeping her back to Lisa Moondaughter. "Perhaps, someday . . ." Getting to her feet, she looked for a moment at Lisa Moondaughter, reclining like an odalisque in the dusky light, her body more eloquent than any words. With a resolve that cost Jennie every ounce of reserve strength in her body, she fled up the path toward the horse pasture. "I'll call you," she flung over her shoulder. A sound tore through the night air, like the wail of a wounded mountain lion—"We don't have a phone."

Back at the ranch, Jennie groomed and watered Firebird in a daze, oblivious to the horse's playful attempts to get her attention. She couldn't think clearly—anxiety over Jeb's dinner, remembrance of Lisa Moondaughter's powerful thighs, and the new things she had learned about tofu all swam together in her head. Firebird whinnied plaintively and she looked at the horse. "Yes," she said, "I know what you're asking. You're wondering what you're doing back here in this cramped stall, instead of gamboling about a grassy meadow. You're yearning for the horsy friends you made this afternoon, longing to butt their withers and rub necks with them. Yes," she said somberly, "I know how you feel."

Jennie heard Barb's hacking cough, and went into her room. The old woman was awake. With a pang, Jennie noted the spots of blood on Barb's handkerchief. "I'll go fix your broth," she murmured, turning away. Barb smiled weakly, and patted the straight-backed chair by the bed. "You're very good to me, Jennie," Barb croaked. "I know it's hard taking care of an old woman like me, especially when you're still a newlywed."

Jennie dropped into the chair and took Barb's hand. "You know I love having you here." For the first time she struggled to explain how things really were between her and Jeb. "It's different than I thought it would be," she said finally. "Sometimes I wonder if maybe my marriage was a mistake, if maybe I could have stayed single and kept working—maybe lived with some other single girls."

A look of pain and weariness crossed Barb's face. "That's what I thought, when I was your age," she said, and then paused for a fit of coughing. "But women friends get married. Horses die. Eventually, even your own body fails you. No, Jennie, be grateful you've got some security—*you* won't end up an old broken-down woman, living on charity."

Wordlessly, Jennie pressed the older woman's hand.

While the broth was on, she wandered into the living room and examined the wedding pictures on the mantel—there were her parents, glowing with pride, her with her bridesmaids. She picked up the portrait of herself and Jeb. The radiant bride in the picture was a stranger to her.

She was still lost in her reverie when she heard a creak behind her. "Hon, you in there?" called Jeb.

She turned to face her husband, the man she'd vowed her life to. He crossed the room in two big strides, and pulled her into his arms with a whoop. "Well, we finally got 'em!"

"The mustangs?" Jennie gasped.

Jeb mistook her horror for delight. "Yep! We had to wait a long time, in that little clearing you told us about, but we finally got 'em!" His rough kiss bruised Jennie's lips. "And guess what else! I found a spot in the County Rest Home for old Barb. It's the best thing for her, really. This way, you won't have to play nurse anymore . . . until you're nursin' my son!" Laughing loudly at his joke, Jeb scooped Jennie's unresisting body in his arms and carried her into the bedroom.

As soon as Jeb had rolled off her and was snoring, Jennie got out of bed and crept outside to look at the captured mustangs. The full moon bathed the corral in its timeless radiance. All was still, except for a lonely dog barking in the distance. The horses were quiet. Some of them, blessedly ignorant of their fate, were asleep where they stood. Others looked at Jennie, their brown eyes full of an ancient animal wisdom. From inside the house came the sound of Jeb snoring.

Jennie knew what she must do. Entering the little room off the stables, she gently shook Barb awake. "Jeb wants to put you in the County Home," she said briefly. Fear leapt into Barb's eyes. "But we have one chance—some friends I'm sure will take us in—if you can ride a little ways—"

Barb pulled herself out of bed with game determination. "I was straddling a horse before you were born. They'll have to pry my cold, dead fingers from the reins before I'll let Jeb or anyone else send me to the County Home! Go saddle up!"

Jennie led Firebird and another horse out of their stalls, then stood for a moment in the shadow of the barn, looking at the mustangs. "Can I turn my back on everything I know," she thought, "from the Bible to *Love Story* to *Cosmopolitan*? Can I ignore the precepts I've been taught by my parents, my teachers, my troop leader?"

But Jennie knew that the old voices no longer held sway over her. She would listen to her own strong woman's voice now. As Jennie moved toward the corral gate, she noticed that a strange hush had fallen over the farm. The horses were all awake, their nostrils flared as they searched the wind for a certain scent—and yes, now Jennie, too, breathed in the pungent odor! Lisa Moondaughter was coming!

She stepped out of the forest with the grace of a mountain lion. Her flimsy, tunic-like garment was transparent in the moonlight, and Jennie bit her lip at the sight of the body she had caressed only a few hours before. Lisa Moondaughter slid across the yard like a liquid brown shadow and fumbled with the latch of the corral. Like a gazelle, Jennie bounded lightly to her side. Placing her hand gently on Lisa Moondaughter's shoulder, she said, "Lisa Moondaughter, I . . ."

Lisa Moondaughter whirled, and her hand gripped Jennie's arm. "Jennie," she breathed, "don't try to stop me!"

"I don't want to stop you, I want to come with you!" Jennie cried.

With an inarticulate strangling sound, like some primeval beast choking, Lisa Moondaughter seemed to cough up a great chunk of pain and sorrow. "I hoped," she said softly when she had caught her breath, "even when I did not dare hope."

And now Jennie saw more women, two of whom were helping Barb mount her horse. "Half a lung?" one was saying. "Western medicine can do nothing. But I have some tea . . ."

The mustangs poured out of the opened corral gate and galloped for the hills. Lisa Moondaughter swung astride the coal-black horse, flashing Jennie a blinding white smile. "Let's ride!"

Jennie ran to Firebird and mounted the waiting horse. "Let's ride," she echoed Lisa Moondaughter. "Ride to freedom!" With a snort, Firebird joined the herd in their race toward the forest.